The Editors

Ever since incurring the wrath of his first editor in 1960 by
making Hitchcock's *Pyscho* his film of the year, **Ciaran Carty**
has been a consistantly independent and passionate commentator
on film and literature, both as a reviewer and through his
interviews with Irish and international artists in *The Sunday
Independent* and later as Arts Editor of *The Sunday Tribune*. His
first book *Robert Ballagh*, a study of the artist, appeared in 1986
and *Confessions of a Sewer Rat*, a personal account of his fight
against censorship and the subsequent development of the Irish
film industry, was published in November, 1995 by New Island
Books. He has been the editor of New Irish Writing since 1989.

Dermot Bolger was born in Dublin in 1959. The author of
five novels (including *The Journey Home* and *A Second Life*),
six plays (including *The Lament for Arthur Cleary* and *April
Bright*) and several collections of poetry, he was the founder and
editor of Raven Arts Press (1977-1992) and is the founder and
executive editor of New Island Books. He has edited such
anthologies as *The Picador Book of Contemporary Irish Fiction*
and has been involved as an adviser on the New Irish Writing
page under the editorship of Ciaran Carty.

THE HENNESSY BOOK
OF
IRISH FICTION

DUBLIN

The Hennessy Book of Irish Fiction
is first published in 1995 by
New Island Books
2, Brookside,
Dundrum Road,
Dublin 14,
Ireland.

The publishers are grateful to all the authors for permission to
reprint these stories; to AP Watt for permission to reprint 'Tell
Me' from Colm O'Gaora's *Giving Ground* (Cape); to Reed
Consumer Books for 'The Last of the Mohicans' from Joseph
O'Connor's *True Believers* (Sinclair-Stevenson); to Poolbeg
Press for 'Widow' from Mary O'Donnell's *Strong Pagans*;
and to Jonathan Cape for 'Thomas Crumlesh 1960-1992: A
Retrospective' from Mike McCormack's *Getting It in the
Head.*

ISBN 1 874597 28 6

New Island Books receives financial assistance from
The Arts Council (**An Chomhairle Ealáion**),Dublin, Ireland.

Cover design by Wilson Hartnell
Typeset by Graphic Resources
Printed in Ireland by Colour Books Ltd.

CONTENTS

New Island Books would like to gratefully acknowledge the financial support of Hennessy Cognac in the publication of this anthology.

The twenty-fifth anniversary of the annual Hennessy Literary Awards is a proud occasion for its sponsors. Inaugurated in 1970 for short stories published in the New Irish Writing page of *The Irish Press*, the Awards, judged each year by two internationally distinguished authors, immediately captured the imagination of readers and writers alike, and quickly established themselves as Ireland's premier literary prize for emerging authors. After *The Irish Press* discontinued New Irish Writing in 1988, the Hennessy Literary Awards were re-launched in 1989, and expanded to include both poetry and fiction first published in New Irish Writing which had found a new home in *The Sunday Tribune*.

Over the past quarter-century many of the then previously unknown recipients of a Hennessy Literary Award have since established themselves among the foremost Irish writers of their generation. This tradition of discovering new and exciting talent has continued over the past seven years in *The Sunday Tribune* as the contents of this anthology readily demonstrate. It is a great pleasure to see this latest generation of writers gathered within these pages. Our involvement with them, and with this unique and world famous platform for Irish writers, has been an honour and a pleasure for both Hennessy Cognac and the entire Hennessy family.

Henri de Pracomtal
President
Jas. Hennessy & Co.
Cognac

These stories are the editors' personal selection from seven years during which New Irish Writing has been published by *The Sunday Tribune*. Often the first — or very early — work of writers who have since established major reputations, they appear here in the order of year in which they were first published, along with the original biographical note, printed at the start of the story. In most cases we have added a current biographical note at the end of each story to bring readers up to date with the authors' careers since their publication in New Irish Writing.

The editors wish to express their gratitude to Anthony Glavin, editor of New Irish Writing in *The Irish Press* (1987-1988), and now literary editor of New Island Books.

Ciaran Carty & Dermot Bolger,
October, 1995

INTRODUCTION

JOSEPH O'CONNOR

The first piece of creative prose I ever wrote in my life was a short story. It was a really good short story, full of beautiful sentences, marvellous insights, wonderful perceptions, juicy dialogue. Actually it was one of the best short stories I've ever read, now that I think of it. The reason for this is very simple. The first short story I ever wrote in my life was a short story by John McGahern.

I don't mean that it was like a John McGahern story, or that it was influenced by a John McGahern story. It actually was a John McGahern story. I was about fifteen at the time and I had found a John McGahern short story in the newspaper my parents often got at home, *The Irish Press*. I should explain to you that something odd was happening to me around then, something disturbing and eerie and not at all pleasant. As if adolescence was not bad enough already (spots, shaving, the inter cert, girls, the Charismatic Renewal) I was discovering in those days that I wanted for some reason to write fiction. But I was also discovering that I couldn't do it. I just couldn't. I would sit on my bed with a copybook and a well-chewed pencil and stare out the window and concentrate very hard on how interesting I was and how nobody in the world really understood my pain. But when it came to turning all of this into highly marketable yet critically acclaimed fiction, I found that I just couldn't do it. I would often re-read that John McGahern story to see if I could figure out how he had done it himself. It all seemed so simple; the story read as if it had taken no effort at all to compose. It read, in fact, as though nobody had ever written it, it read as if it had just somehow grown on the page. (I had not yet learnt the important truth that the things which are easiest to read are the

9

very things which were hardest to write.) But when I tried to write myself the words wouldn't come, although the desire to find them was so gnawingly oppressive it was almost akin to a hunger. So one day in desperation I sat down on the bed and actually wrote out that John McGahern story word for word in my school copybook. I was determined to write a short story that day, you see, so write one I darn well did.

I suppose I felt at the time that the act of writing out the story made it in some fundamental way mine. I just wanted to know what that feeling was like, to write out a whole story from beginning to end. I suppose what I was doing was the literary equivalent of the carbuncular aspiring pop star strumming a tennis racket and sneering into the bedroom mirror with the collar of his school shirt turned up. Shortly after that day, I wrote out the story again, only this time I inserted some sentences of my own. It felt like an incredibly cheeky if not downright taboo thing to be doing, but God, it was fun! From then on, I would write that story out quite often, sometimes putting in my own characters, my own paragraphs, my own experiences, sometimes cutting out whole chunks of gorgeous John McGahern prose, until eventually I noticed that the story really was mine now. Slowly, inexorably, all trace of John McGahern had disappeared, ghostlike into the ether. The story wasn't very good or anything. It was screamingly bad, in fact, but at least it was mine. There it was in the copybook, I had written my first short story almost by accident. So I owe a lot to both John McGahern and *The Irish Press* for helping me get off to some kind of start with fiction. I also owe them a lot for the fact that I spectacularly failed my mathematics exam in the inter cert that year — I was writing bloody awful stories when I should have been doing my homework — and thus avoided a career in chartered or even certified accountancy.

There is a lot of talk in Ireland about the importance of the short story form. Wherever two or three Irish-American literary academics are gathered, the names of Sean O'Faolain and Liam

O'Flaherty and Frank O'Connor are reverently invoked like some sort of latterday Holy Trinity. We Irish are very good at the short story, we are constantly telling ourselves, as though having an Irish passport automatically entitles the bearer to be able to produce a really startling neo-Joycean epiphany in two shakes of a lamb's tail. The truth, however, is a little more complex. Writing good short stories is not easy. So many short stories are imitative, or tricksy, or twee, or boring, or sentimental, or lacking in resonance, or just plain bad. "All we have," wrote the great American short story writer, Raymond Carver, "are the words, and they had better be the right ones, with the punctuation in the right places so that they can best say what they are meant to say. If the words are heavy with the writer's own unbridled emotions, or if they are imprecise and inaccurate for some other reason — if the words are in any way blurred — the reader's eyes will slide right over them and nothing will be achieved....The short story writer's task is to invest the glimpse with all that is in his power."

This kind of writing, the kind which invests the mere glimpse of experience with the power of fiction, is hard and demanding and requires great skill and endless work. Not everybody can do it. And even the people who can do it have their problems, because having done it, it's not always easy to get it published. This is one of the reasons why the Irish short story is in a bit of trouble these days. There are very few places to publish stories in Ireland now, and not many in England either. Up until quite recently, mainstream publishers at least used to regard the production of a book of stories as being an odd kind of literary apprenticeship, something which an Irish writer had to be allowed do before he or she would consent to become upwardly mobile, join the first division and write a novel. Nowadays they don't even bother doing that much, or that little. Short stories do not sell, the line goes; nobody is interested in short stories. This isn't actually true, by the way, but then mainstream publishing has so much on its mind these days, what with so many supermodels and TV presenters wanting to crown their glorious careers by fictionalizing their neuroses and calling the result a novel, or, at least, by allowing someone else to fictionalize their neuroses for them, in return for a fat ghostwriter's fee.

I guess that's why The Hennessy Awards and The New Irish Writing page in *The Sunday Tribune* are so important. The page provides the largest regular popular audience for new short fiction and poetry anywhere in Ireland (or Britain, for that matter).

And the awards are designed — as so few literary awards are these days — to encourage the writer who is just starting out, rather than to reward the established writer who really doesn't need the recognition, the kudos, the money, or, perhaps most importantly, the encouraging clap on the back that winning a Hennessy Award provides, the simple statement of confidence which implies that you're not totally wasting your time trying to write.

The page was started by the writer and editor David Marcus in *The Irish Press* twenty-five years ago now. He published a new story and a few new poems every week. This represented a huge and important commitment to the work of new writers. Whatever else happened, you could be sure that fifty-two brand new stories would be published every year in Ireland, to take their chances in the world and fight for their slice of public affection. Some of those writers have been forgotten now, but a considerable number have gone on to national and international acclaim. Indeed, it is very difficult indeed to think of more than three or four important Irish writers who emerged in the seventies or eighties without being published as tyros in the New Irish Writing page of *The Irish Press*. This, it seems to me, is a wonderful thing. In a society which rarely tired of trotting out meaningless platitudes about the tremendous importance of writers, David Marcus actually did something concrete to help them, and he did it week after week, year after year, and the stories just kept pouring out.

In 1989, some time after *The Irish Press* had dropped the New Irish Writing page, *The Sunday Tribune* started to publish it and to take over administration of The Hennessy Awards, under the enlightened stewardship of the paper's excellent arts editor, Ciaran Carty. For the first year, a story was published every week. After that the page appeared once a month, but focused exclusively on writers yet to publish in book form. It has continued to do for six years now, no mean achievement in the competitive world of newspaper publishing. Again, many of the writers whose work has appeared during that time — Hugo Hamilton, Colm O'Gaora, Colum McCann, Marina Carr, and Mary O'Donnell amongst them — have either simultaneously or subsequently established themselves as part of the most vibrantly energetic generation of Irish writers to have appeared for many decades.

In February 1989, my own story "The Last of the Mohicans" was published in *The Sunday Tribune*. It was my first published story. In November that year I won the Hennessy award for the best first published story and then the overall award for the best new Irish writer of the year. It was a lovely day and we all expressed our gratitude to the Hennessy people for their many years of generous and intelligent sponsorship by consuming as much of their high quality (and so reasonably priced) product as was physically possible and then stealing the cutlery. (OK, OK, so I made that last bit up.) But it was an important day for me, because I made up my mind at some point during that wonderful day that for better or worse I wouldn't ever do anything else but write.

Thus I owe so much to the New Irish Writing page and to Ciaran Carty personally that it's impossible for me to tell you about it here without getting a trembling lip. I'm not talking about winning the prize now — although that was very pleasant — I'm talking about just getting published. The truth is that I was on the point of giving up writing completely when my first story appeared. I had been writing for several years without any success at all, without even one publication. My girl friend and I would spend whole days photocopying my stories and sending them out to as many newspapers and literary magazines as we could think of, and one by one the envelopes would flow back through the letterbox, morning after morning, an unrelenting torrent of refusal. Many people who don't write fiction themselves seem to regard writing as a glamorous or an exciting activity. In fact, it is often hard, often boring, lonely, frustrating work, and in the early months of 1989 I had really had enough of it. I felt defeated, ground-down, hopeless. At the time I'm describing to you, I had a file of rejection letters as thick as an airport hardback and a five-hundred-page monster of an experimental first novel which, I was just realizing, simply did not work, which, in point of fact, had just keeled over, kissed its backside goodbye and died in terrible agony. And then my story was published! There it was, in *The Tribune* one Sunday morning, where real people could read it, like it, moan about it, hate it, whatever. But at least it was there. In the months after its appearance I wrote more than I ever had before. I threw out my five-hundred-page, neo-Marquezian, sub-Beckettian, crypto-Joycean experimental masterpiece, took the character from *The Tribune* short story, Eddie Virago, began to try to strip down my writing, to make it less pretentious and more direct, began to find my own voice and to write what would turn out to be my first real novel, *Cowboys And Indians*. That book was published in 1991. It is an absolute matter of fact — although this is a confession that fills me with dread — that it never would have been written, and, indeed, I would not still be writing now, if Ciaran Carty had not published that short story of mine on the New Irish Writing page in February 1989.

I can only hope that the writers included in the present anthology are as encouraged by publication as I was myself, for this is a deeply impressive selection which is eclectic in tone, funny, disturbing, touching, linguistically playful, full of the sheer wonder at the everyday with which the finest of short stories resound, and we need these writers to keep going, to keep telling us their stories. Some of those included here are already carving out very considerable reputations; others quite clearly have the kind of insistently original voices which will be well worth listening out for in the years and decades to come. I wish them all joy and continued success in the daily struggle towards what Raymond Carver called "getting the words right". The words are all we have in the end, he said. Long may these writers persevere in that knowledge. And long may the New Irish Writing Page and The Hennessy Awards continue to celebrate the power of the short story to speak for our time, the miraculous, fundamental, moral importance of the words.

1988

GOODBYE TO THE HURT MIND

HUGO HAMILTON

Hugo Hamilton received a £2,000 Arts Council Bursary this year and an earlier story, 'The Suspicion of Grief', which was first published in New Irish Writing, has been selected for the forthcoming Faber Introductions series due out next February. He has just finished his first novel. Born in Dublin in 1953, he grew up speaking German and Irish—his mother was German, his father an Irish-language enthusiast. "I only learned English later in school. No English was allowed in the house. It made me value it."

You're full a shite ... he said looking straight over at me.

When you hear that coming in a slick Belfast accent, there's no mistake. Nobody was looking for trouble. Nobody had said a word to him. He seemed very drunk and his dark eyes looked across at me either with intense rage or intense stupor.

I said nothing. I half knew the woman he was with, Helen Connors. She looked at him reproachfully, and frowned at the floor beneath him. Graham, she pleaded. What are you saying? He was drunk; slumped down on his elbows. But he kept staring at me. We were all sitting at this large round table listening to the band playing. His eyes wouldn't leave me. The candle at the centre of the table seemed to make everything look darker. It cast a black wavering circular shadow beneath itself on the table. Gave Helen Connors a black line for her cleavage. Even the wine looked black in the glasses; black as H-Block flags or black plastic bags. And candles seem to give everyone such pale flesh-tones, like degraded election posters gone pale with age. The music was just about loud enough to pretend nothing was happening.

Full a shite ... he repeated.

How long can you ignore that? I looked away; pretended to be desperately interested in the band at that moment. But you can't ignore it. Because you then begin to think, maybe he's half right. Maybe he knows something.

The Belfast accent keeps ringing in your ear. It's like tinnitus. You can never be sure either what they're saying up there. Was it 'shite' or 'shout' he said? By the sound of it, so many words seemed interchangeable in Northern Ireland. Paisley used to shout a lot. Twice, I've been up there for a bit of fishing and they all keep shouting about Fashion ... fashion ... fashion.

I couldn't help taking another look at your man Graham, but he was still staring at me. Why me, I thought. Beside the candle on the table there was a blue menu card jammed between pepper and salt and a small vase containing a single daffodil. This was repeated on every table.

Janet asked me to collect her mother from the hairdresser. Her mother always pretends at the hairdresser's that I am her lover. Here's my Romeo, she says. I wait in the cane chairs without picking up one of the magazines on the glass table. They offer me coffee. No thanks! The mirrors are also framed with cane. The image must have been decided on from the beginning; cane surrounds along with red towels. I can half see Janet's mother's face in the mirror. Somebody sweeps up the cut hair around her on the floor. There is an ad on the radio for late-night shopping. The oval mirror is held to the back of Janet's mother's head and the back of the head must go nodding into infinity along the mirrors. I have to remember to tell her that her hair looks great. Janet's mother links arms as we leave the hairdresser's and the girls smile. The scent of hairspray fills the car.

Helen Connors was the first to make a move. She stood up and put her coat on. Then gave Belfast a slap on the shoulder with the back of her hand and said: Come on you. Treats him like a schoolboy. Up you get! He is footless; makes the bar look like a ferry. She left him propped for a moment against a chair while she plunged down towards us to pick up her bag, looking at me with a half-smile before she steered him out through the gaps in the tables, past the stage and through the door out into the street.

As soon as he was gone, they started talking about him. They said he was manky. Mouldy. Out of it. Somebody told me he worked as a photographer. Not long after that, I left as well and my ears were buzzing when I stepped out into the street. When I got home the house seemed unusually quiet. In the kitchen, the sandwiches and flasks stood ready for school in the morning. I sat down and switched the radio on and refused to think about the next day. I knew Janet was already half way through it.

The next time I saw Helen Connors, she was standing naked in a field beside a tree. There was another photograph of her sitting naked in a large empty room looking straight at you through an open door. There was no mistake; it was Helen Connors without her clothes on. I recognised her immediately. His name was there too: Graham Delargy. The rest of the photographs in the exhibition were of helicopters or soldiers or walls with graffiti.

I had never imagined Helen Connors like that with dusty circular shadings around her nipples and I couldn't look at her any longer because breasts are like eyes, bogus eyes. So I walked around looking at other pictures. But when I came back to her, there were two women examining her.

Nobody likes repetition. Why can't things happen just once?

When Janet's mother comes around to dinner on Tuesdays, she wears her fur coat. She likes to pretend this is a special occasion, her first ever visit to the house. I hand her a glass of sherry. She takes my arm and says to Janet: You don't mind if I borrow your husband for a moment. Janet's mother tells me about a famous dentist she could have married. He was mad about her. Extremely intelligent man. He asked her to marry him many times but she turned him down. Gave him back the ring he once gave her; they were on the train at the time going from Limerick to Dublin when he accepted the ring back and then threw it out the window of the carriage.

Why didn't she marry him, I ask? But she can't answer that. Usually people want to know if she remembered the spot where he threw the ring out. Did anyone go back to look for it. She laughs. That was an expensive ring too.

After dinner, Janet asks me to put on a waltz for her mother. Dancing rinses out resentment, her mother says. She likes 'The Blue Danube' best. She once stayed in Vienna. It was in Vienna that she learned to dance. Mere contact with the city was enough.
— *Einmal hin, einmal her, rund herum, das ist nicht schwer.* Janet's mother wants me to dance with her. I'm much taller than she is. But not firm enough. Too stiff. Too stiff. Ah, you're no use at all, she says. A man should lead. Are you a man?

Janet dances with one of the children. Their movements are exaggerated and comic. This is a repetition of last week.

I was bound to meet him again at some stage. Delargy. When I did, some months later on one of those fishing trips up north, it was a bit of a shock. I had no idea who else was going on the trip and we both happened to be invited by the same people; mutual friends. He was introduced to me as Graham Delargy and we had to pretend we had never met before.

From first eye contact there seemed to be an unspoken arrangement between us not to bring up anything from the past. I had to pretend I didn't know he was a photographer. I had to laugh and respond to his conversation like any new acquaintance. He had to ensure he didn't appear to be apologetic or considerate. When he held the door of the bar open for me, it had to appear natural as though he would have done it for any stranger. When I bought him a pint, he quickly bought one back at the next opportunity so as to keep a surface equality. And of course we couldn't say a word about Helen Connors.

Next morning on the way down to the lake from the lodging-house, things seemed less strained; less like a conspiracy. There was the weather to talk about, and fishing conditions. You get on better with declared opponents than you do with declared friends. When I got into the same boat with him and accidentally pushed against him, it almost appeared as though I had finally decided to take revenge and push him into the lake. Out on the lake, it's every man for himself. There's not much to talk about anyway. Anglers are solipsists. There was the irrational anxiety that hooks and lines would become entangled. And later, I reached for a sandwich in my bag and discovered it was his bag I was fumbling at and quickly withdrew my hand.

In the bar that evening, everybody got drunk. Delargy more than anyone else. We were getting on very well. Then, as if to wipe the slate clean, Delargy put him arm around one of the other anglers who happened to be talking too much and said: You're full a shite - you scabby bastard. Inverse flattery. It's the way angling friends are in Ireland; insulted if you stop insulting them. The way a fish would feel insulted if you didn't eat it after you went and caught it.

Janet likes to repeat things. She can relate the same story twice or three times over in successive phone calls. When I read a book,

I hold it so that it looks almost unread when I'm finished. Janet cracks the spine and leaves books face down on the sofa while she's on the phone.

Janet remembers odd things. Names of people and street names. She still knows the name of the shopkeeper at the end of the road in Wood Green when we lived in London. He was from Pakistan. I'd have to ask her. She still knows the names of all the streets around there and all the names on the bells of each flat in the house. I remember the upturned ice cream cone beneath the seat of the bus the day we went to visit her uncle. She could tell me the name of the pub we drank in. The Elephant and Castle?

Janet hates bringing the car to the garage for repairs. She says it reminds her of a gynaecological examination every time a mechanic starts poking around underneath the bonnet. Janet never remembers to check the oil in the car because that's something I remember.

It is me who collects the car from the garage in the afternoon. It is me who first grips the oily steering wheel when I get into the car. It is the mechanic who sees me searching for tissues and points knowingly to a large drum of blotting paper on the wall. It is both Janet and her mother who are at the hairdresser's today. It is me who remembers to say that they both have lovely hair.

Long after Janet's mother is gone home again, Janet asks me if I remember the name of a pub in Kensington. I ask her if she knows the colours of Lufthansa. She asks if I know the name of the bakery on the High Street. I ask her what date internment was introduced. What is the capital of Fiji? Who was the bass guitarist with the Rolling Stones?

It is me who lies in bed awake and cannot avoid remembering the name of the garage: Huet Motors. I continually see petrol pumps and the greasy interior of the workshop. It is me who thinks the bed is on the floor of the workshop. It is Janet who embraces me.

Mind you don't get any oil on my hair.

There's nothing in the world but the thought in my head.

The last time I met him was outside Trinity College, along the railings. It must have been around five o'clock in the evening. People were going home from work. The windows of passing buses were steamed up. The passengers upstairs had cleared circles with the sleeves of their coats; enough to look out at the street and the railings of Trinity and the people walking by. Delargy stopped me and asked me what I was doing. I can never describe what I'm doing.

Come on you bugger, he said. Let's murder a pint.

On our way to the pub, we passed lots of people waiting for buses. As usual, there was a man selling the evening papers at the corner of Westmoreland Street. As usual, I remember the names of streets when I pass through them and forget them again as soon as they are behind me.

He told me he was getting out. Australia. He had organised a job over there in Sydney.

You bastard!

There was a mate of his already over there with a house on a beach near the city.

You dirty bastard!

In the pub he kept talking about Australia. Fishing. Hunting. Women. Dynamite. From time to time I had to look at my watch. It's goodbye to Ireland, he kept saying. Goodbye to the hurt mind. Then he ordered more and more pints so that we lost count. Come on, let's make a disgrace of ourselves, he said.

The barman kept laughing at him. Told him to make sure and put on a condom when he got off the plane in Sydney, like a good lad.

I had to carry him home. He kept shouting and mumbling. In the door of Burger King, he shouted: Goodbye to the hurt mind, but there was no reaction except a few puzzled stares.

As we arrived around at Helen Connors' house, he fell asleep on her doorstep. He couldn't even make it into the hallway. I had to pretend I had never seen her body naked before. I had to pretend everything was a surprise. We carried him in and laid him on the bed. I took off his boots. She took off his jacket.

Since this story appeared, Hugo Hamilton has published three acclaimed novels set in Germany, **Surrogate City** *(1990),* **The Last Shot** *(1991) — which won the Rooney Prize for Irish Literature — and* **The Love Test** *(1995). His first collection of short stories,* **Dublin Where the Palm Trees Grow** *is due from Faber in January 1996.*

1988

WIDOW

MARY O'DONNELL

A graduate in German and Philosophy from Maynooth College, Mary O'Donnell has taken a career break from teaching to devote herself full-time to writing. She was twice a prize-winner at Listowel Writers' Week, a runner-up in the Patrick Kavanagh Poetry Award and a 3rd Prizewinner in last year's Bloodaxe Poetry Competition. Some of her poetry will be published soon in Poetry Oxford. She featured in the RTE 'Just a Thought' programme each morning last week and is a frequent broadcaster. 'Widow', which she is now adapting as a screen play, is her fifth story to appear in New Irish Writing.

The coffin disappeared quietly behind the curtain in the crematorium at Glasnevin. She had seen to everything, from organising the service to comforting stunned relatives when she herself stood tearless. There were no feelings with which to grapple. It was an unmediated cerebral acceptance. Afterwards, they crowded around, pressing her shoulders occasionally, clasping her hands intently, and she sensed their compassion, aware that their pain would be indignant and short-lived. "So young...," someone behind her sighed. "It's always the same —" the voice went on. "In the prime of life — he had so much to achieve..." before petering out to an asthmatic sob.

Back at the house she breathed easily, relieved that it was over. The women moved around her, passing plates piled high with salads, and dessert-bowls which wobbled with pavlovas and cheesecakes. You could always depend on the women in time of bereavement. Lisa spoke to all her comforters, said what she knew they would wish to hear, indifferent to their presence, whether they came or went, spoke the words which would soothe them in their sympathetic anguish. "Don't know how I'll manage," she shrugged her shoulders helplessly at Marian. "I can't believe it — I really can't take it in..." The friend shifted comfortingly. "Of course you can't darling, of course you can't," touching her arm familiarly. "But you know we're all with you in this — you know that, don't you?" Lisa nodded. And anytime — anytime — " Marian gripped her arm even harder this time, "that you need to talk — you know what I mean — just *shout*." Lisa looked at her. "Thanks," she replied in as grateful a tone as she could muster.

The place smelt like a party. People laughed, then suddenly checked themselves. It had been a massive haemorrhage which struck on the way home from the city, right in the centre of his chest. He had managed to drive the rest of the journey, arrived gasping and white. Later that evening, he had died in the hospital theatre. Booze and cigar smoke wraithed the air. She sat back on the old leather sofa which still bore the green and blue woven blanket they'd bought one year in Morocco, and inhaled the atmosphere. It could have been one of their openings, or even the small exhibition they'd held in the studio the previous spring, when small hordes of art lovers had trooped across the cracked yellow tiling that led to the annexe behind their house. The art lovers could never decide how to behave, she thought a little amusedly. Whether to appear silent and awe-struck, as if they were in a temple of worship on the site of an ancient deity, or whether loud nonchalance was best. The terracotta exhibition, as she'd referred to it since then, had been a mix of refined and sometimes awkward silences, and elegant outbursts of laughter, depending on who was there. Much like the funeral, she thought. The aorta had ruptured. She played with the word 'aorta', tongued it around her mouth. The simplicity of the words had astonished her with their weight of intent, the television soap opera line "I'm sorry Mrs. Jordan — we could do nothing..."

She observed an artist friend on the other side of the room as his lips rounded on a forkful of food. For a moment, her thoughts blurred, lost their razor-sharp coldness. Was it a party after all? Mental focus hardened once more, and the discomfiting sense of fracture left. They were celebrating death after all, mollifying what they did not fully understand, by eating, drinking and laughing, in the hope that they could frighten it away. That the spectre would not come too soon. It was the dance of death, a courting of favours. By celebrating, whilst imagining they were mourning one of their number, they were in fact preening themselves that they had survived, and could escort death to the very door, perhaps send him on his way, far from the brittle peripheries of their lives.

Marian stayed for a week. Lisa did not sleep any night, which came as no surprise. It was part of the rite. She was alone. She would grow accustomed to aloneness. Initially she decided that the best way to accentuate that aloneness and get the painful aspects sorted out, was to leave Alan's bits and pieces exactly as they lay. The steel edge of grief had to be faced head-on. People were kind, and not just for the sake of it, but sensitive too, perceptive of her needs.

Spring had come early that year, and with it an inner exasperation with such gentle winds, such warmth, such frenetic blossoming everywhere. The world spilt its kindnesses on her with a cruelty she had never before experienced. Her calmness and the routine quietness with which she coped disturbed the family. Yet there seemed no point in tearing her hair before them. Life could always be reduced to coping situations. Still, there were times of admission when she longed to race to the top of Killiney Hill and beat her chest while she screamed out at the sea. There were certainly times when the coast road and the broken paths which led to the shore might provide a sinister invitation.

Gradually, she disassembled Alan's belongings. He'd had masses of underwear which she discovered when rummaging through the back of the airing-cupboard one day. She had thrust her face into a pile of vests, disappointed when they didn't smell of him. Just washing powder, fresh laundry, warmth. His jackets had hung for months before she even looked at them. They too had had their odour, a tweedy mixture of tobacco and oils from the ancient brown one he used to wear in the studio. More delicate aromas from the other two. Aftershave. The smell of a man. That was when she first began to clench her fists and stand silently for minutes. The smell of a man. It was, she knew, the real beginning of her term. Lonely as opposed to alone. A place like Alcatraz. This was the start and there might be no escape. She had entered the studio one day after work. The gnawing and yearning had begun in earnest. It was as if she were in solitary confinement, as if she could observe herself doing time with grief, could map her own progress day by day.

After much fiddling with the key, the rusted lock yielded. Inside, everything lay beneath an indistinct swathe of white sheets. She wondered if Marian had covered the canvases during the week she stayed. She began to remove the sheets, sneezed as she did so, then opened the cracked yellow shutters that kept the room in shadow. Sunlight streamed promisingly into the place and she stood for a moment idly transfixed by minor maelstroms of dust that spiralled everywhere. The canvases lay stacked against the walls, finished and unfinished. All oils. He'd finished with acrylics the previous year, she remembered. "No subtlety," he'd commented at the time, "all cut and corner — which is grand if you're a draughtsman." She recalled how he'd stood back appraisingly from the piece on which he was then working, his remark hanging noncommittally on the air between them. "Oils," he'd said then, cleaning his brushes half-teasingly, "are like women. They flow into everything, mould their characteristics to any mood, defy rigidity of thought..." He'd stood there absently, watching the canvas before him, as if he were addressing it rather than her.

The last piece lay unfinished, just as he'd left it the day he died. It was the head and shoulders of a young man. The model had come to the funeral, was extravagantly and noticeably distraught. She recalled the face, twisted in an expression of near-despair. There it was again, she thought, but quite different. Alan had caught the seed of humour in the boy, had gained access to the secrets of his imagination. The young face before her was unsmiling, yet laughter lay not far behind the skin of his softly contoured face. It was the eyes that registered, forcing her to smile. She turned from the canvas almost angrily. This was where *he* had worked. She could remember him more vividly than ever, stood lost in imagining how it had been. The peace of the studio, the sitter usually reverent and co-operative for those few hours while she read in the sunchair near the window, time whittled to a caprice of brush strokes, or the sharp *sshish* sound of the palette knife as he textured an image, blended a colour. The need rose in her sharply then. A terrible need. One which nobody ever mentioned, which Marian always seemed to avoid. Recollection brought a rush of desire yet again. This was where he'd work. This was where they'd occasionally made love, beneath uncurtained windows, bright in the sunlight yet tucked out of sight. This was where he was most himself, most the man. Within their own context, they'd had what seemed now to be indefinite freedom.

Two weeks later, she'd seduced three men of her acquaintance. It had been remarkably simple, she discovered, as if they'd half-expected it, were well-primed for invitations such as hers. But then, she reasoned, wasn't that what they assumed about a widow-woman, especially a young one? Couldn't the old peasant instincts always be relied on where a woman on her own was concerned? What exacerbated her regret was that it had provided no relief at all. Unsatisfactory couplings all three. The longing rose more intensely, biting with a ferocity which almost frightened her. She made an appointment with a doctor. "Oh, sex-withdrawal," he remarked, "absolutely normal — you'll get used to it."

Marian was incredulous. "You mean you've slept with *three*?"

"I'm on my own now, aren't I?"

"I suppose so," Marian considered doubtfully. "But — d'you really feel like it so soon after...I mean how can you feel that way now...?"

Did she feel like it? It was all she could do to avoid lingering on any attractive man she saw, even on the streets. She was more aware than ever of slender muscularity, of slim thighs, of fine, young skin. She was not merely hungry. She was famine-stricken.

"Best take it easy though," Marian warned confidentially, "I mean, they might begin to think you're anybody's..." Again, her voice faded as she struggled with words, distaste and incomprehension etched clearly on her features.

The party was three weeks later. "Bring someone," Marian had urged accommodatingly. Lisa considered. "No. I'll come alone." She'd had no sleep for three nights, felt raw and sour as morning sunlight streamed unobligingly into her face where she stood in the hallway. She was beginning to get the picture. Her arrival with a partner would present no difficulties to a hostess. She hardened within. Let them sweat it out with the newly bereaved woman. The woman on her own. "OK. If you're sure," Marian had sighed. "I'm sure. See you Friday."

She wore black. Simple black which plunged gently at the back. From her ears hung the old red-gold earrings which Alan had bought her in Turkey for their anniversary one year. Her dark hair was swept high in a pony-tail, revealing a long and elegant neck. She felt poised, yet strangely angry. They had travelled so many roads in those twelve years, had taken trains and planes, had lugged backpacks to bright, sunny places. She listed the countries mentally. Turkey, Morocco, Tunisia, Yugoslavia, Crete, France, Italy, Germany. The house was cluttered in a slight way with minor mementos, bits of carved wood, porcelain, camel leather, rugs and blankets. She did not know why she had come to the party. Everything about her, everything she knew, was rooted in the past. But she greeted the husband of an acquaintance with a bonhomie which she did not feel, realised that she wanted to cause discomfort. She would do what they imagined and feared, what the limitation of imagination allowed them to see. Aware that some of the women would pity her, that she would have been the occasional subject of one of Marian's lunches, she knew also that tonight their sympathy would metamorphose into rigid suspicion.

Suddenly she saw him, demanded of Marian that they be introduced. Marian had drifted competently between groups of people who clustered together like constellations. Stars in their own heaven. And who was she? Dog-star Sirius, bright, bright, full of need and loneliness, attached to nobody, to nothing but a past. He was young looking. Before Marian could do anything, he had approached of his own volition. Certain she hadn't seen him at any previous gathering about town, she took the initiative by telling him so. "Bill," he said by way of introduction. He was slim, even bony. Almost immediately she noticed his hands. The left one was scarred below the knuckles, the skin around the healed wound smooth and sallow. His hair was moppish, curls instead of the geometric square so beloved of men in their twenties. His watch was sellotaped together and read five past three. "How d'you tell the time?" she asked impulsively. "Time? — Oh, I manage — I look at the sun," he smiled, shrugging his shoulders. She extended her hand towards him. He looked at it for a moment, and for a split second she thought he was not going to respond, but he took it, brushed it quickly and matter-of-factly.

A women she'd never met approached. "'Scuse me, 'scuse me," she pushed towards Lisa. "Just wanted to say how...how terribly..." She struggled to form her words, "*sorry* I was about your husband, really sorry, really sorry." Lisa murmured acceptance, dropping her voice as she always did when people spoke of Alan. The woman held on to her arm irritatingly. "If you're ever stuck, y'know, if you ever need someone to chat to — must be hard." She removed the woman's hand in what she hoped was a discreet gesture. "No," she answered mutely. "It's not so bad now, but thanks for being so kind." She smiled at the stranger, hoping she would go. Bill looked on, his expression intensifying. Again she caught her forearm, this time holding fast. Lisa knew the type. If you smile at them you've had it, they come on even more strongly, grow more invasive by the second. "I know what it's like," the woman whispered wetly, "I know what you're goin' through..." This time, she removed the hand more roughly than she had intended, and her voice was loud. "Yes," she replied clearly, "I'm sure you do. Now thank you so much. Don't let me hold you up." Her back rolled with perspiration, resentment and frustration beating a rhythm in her brain, hands rattling the steel bars of a cage. The woman's face darkened as she were about to become abusive. Her mouth opened and her eyes narrowed.

"Can I fill your glass?" It was Bill. Thank God, thank God, she thought, as the woman relented when he touched her elbow and proceeded to lead her across the room. Lisa's legs had begun to tremble. Just the sort of thing she could do without. She swallowed as her throat swelled with self-pity, and tribes of unnameable angers assaulted. She glanced quickly around. Marian had heard the conversation, stood with a couple who looked casually in her direction from time to time. Taking her drink, she sat down near the door, where the night air swirled in soothingly. She turned her face towards the draught, unsure as never before, full of a torment that could never have been anticipated. She surveyed the crowd with hatred. Threads of conversation drifted towards her, "... badminton...ladies team...after a coffee-morning...new exhibition in the Douglas Hyde." The voices rose and fell, but there was no solace in the tide of sounds, only a gathering tempest that must surely explode. They were all obscene, herself included. Dressed in bright leathers, animal skins, their arms, ears and hands heavy with jewellery, the men just as much part of the conspiracy, careful social animals, fenced-in wildcats who could purr smugly because they were well-fed, well-dressed, well-sired.

She jumped at the touch of a hand on her shoulder. "Sorry about that," Bill apologised. "Steered her back to the gin. A few more won't make any difference," he grinned. "Thanks," she replied dully. "No problem," he responded. "Not what you need I imagine — this is supposed to be a party, not a funeral — ." He broke off suddenly, as if he'd said something inappropriate. They looked at one another for a long time. His face reddened. Suddenly her laughter exploded, and finally he laughed too, an easy humour in his eyes. He was an unknown quantity, a person actually capable of embarrassment. Nevertheless, after they had exchanged phone numbers, she left early and alone.

That night she stretched out as fully as possible in the double bed, felt the chill corners of unexplored territory with her feet. This was how it would be, this was a sense of the future. A widow at thirty-five. Widow. The word revolted her, bounced tenaciously about as if forcing her to accept its implications. It reminded her of the spider, the one that poisoned its mate after copulation, suggested blackness, sorrowful *mater melancholias*, women who would never have a man beside them again, who would never enjoy a man's company or friendship for fear of what people would think. Widow. In the early Christian Church they were a special class of pious women, who performed certain duties approved of by their elders, duties which kept them out of mischief, away from other women's men. Bill, she felt certain, may have thought he recognised easy prey. Yet he had done nothing about it. She shouted out in the darkness, swinging her fists back to the headboard of the bed, hammering till her hands hurt. In spite of everything, she felt no different. Desire refused to evaporate with death. It would have been convenient had it done so, had all her lusts and wants gone down to the pyre along with Alan's body instead of remaining with her like an ambivalent inheritance, festering within, contorting her perception. Eventually she slept, aware that the birds had begun to sing, that the first buses were lurching down the road.

It was a mistake to mention Bill to Marian, even if unavoidable.

"For God's sake be careful — you shouldn't take such risks — and so soon — ."

"It's six months now — don't be pious."

"I'm not. Just worried about you...by the way I'm having a lunch next week — can you come?" she asked, changing the subject.

"When?"

"Wednesday."

"No. I'll be with Bill." He had sounded surprised when she rang, but the light voice betrayed no displeasure. He was, if nothing, curious. Marian picked up a magazine and flicked through it sullenly. Lisa smiled. Marian liked to call all the shots. Without meaning to, she enjoyed an element of control in her role as chief comforter of the bereaved.

"Gotta go. Work to do at the studio."

"Alan's?" Perplexity flickered on her face.

"What was Alan's. I'm converting it — I'll rent it to a couple of artists. There's room for at least three — no point in having it lie there."

Younger than ever, she thought as she opened the door. He had brought flowers. Carnations, spicy and aromatic, as if he knew. She would accept full responsibility. He had done nothing, had made no move towards her. He stood in the middle of the hallway, awkward-looking, bonier than she remembered.

"It must be strange," he commented.

"What?"

"All this — ," he gestured with the scarred hand, taking in the whole house. "You're not used to it — by yourself I mean," he added. Simple words stung most, especially kind ones. She answered with a 'No' that was almost a whisper.

"Want to see around?" she asked lightly, in an attempt to recover her equilibrium. "I've lots of books,' she added nervously. He nodded. She brought him through the house, from the black-and-white-tiled kitchen with its scrubbed wooden table on which stood a chipped vase of lilac, to her workroom, and beside it, what had been Alan's.

He was discreet, like a gentle but rangy-looking wolf that knows its limits. They ate in the kitchen, where it was bright and warm, and drank a bottle of red wine. Later, she felt the response in the pressure of his lips on her cheek, but also caution, an unwillingness to assume. It might not be a mistake at all, she thought, dimly recalling Marian's reaction the previous week. They undressed self-consciously in the bedroom. "I'm scared," she laughed. "Me too," he replied, stroking her shoulder. His body was smooth and supple, so beautiful it almost made her weep before they lay down. She rose easily to a climax, her arms and legs full of his smoothness, his hairless body, his avid movements. But just as she let herself go, no sooner had the first moment of release torn relievingly, than it broke. The tempest. What she had feared and anticipated.

She was blinded by the wrench of memory. At first he misunderstood her cries. Gradually it dawned. She clung to him, clawed like an animal tearing the earth. Her mouth opened as she let out a long cry. It was a cry of primal grief. He made no attempt to release her, to be rid of her, but held on. He was tender and gentle. He stroked her head, kissed her temples where the tears streamed into her hair, whispered in the hollows of her neck. Words that meant nothing in particular. But the voice was human and the skin was human. The body was a man's, a kind man's. She caressed him again, and sobbed even more, his name, not Bill's, but the old name, the other name, the lost name that she could never utter again. Still he didn't move. Still he stayed close, his arms cradling her, his hands and mouth enacting a rite of consolation, drawing her on, bearing her as gradually she wept less and it was only when she had screamed the name twice more at the moment of release as it came again, that she let herself rage at him for having left, that she cursed Alan with serpentine venom. It was her turn to mollify the dark spectre, her turn to court favours of the unknown, to escort a sensed but unseen figure beyond the portals of desire.

Much later, they slept. She awoke in the middle of the night, felt him beside her, curled loosely in sleep. The chains had been sundered. Doors flew open, door upon door, leading out to a horizon, a sense of space that would not be ruptured. For the first time, she was calm.

*"Widow" was later published in Mary O'Donnell's debut collection of stories **Strong Pagans**. Her first novel, **The Light-Makers** was an Irish best-seller and her second novel, **Virgin and the Boy**, will be published in 1996. She has also published two collections of poetry and served as Writer-in-Residence at University College Dublin.*

1989

THE LAST OF THE MOHICANS

JOSEPH O'CONNOR

*Joe O'Connor was born in Dublin in 1963 and graduated from UCD in 1986 with a first class MA in English. He has reported from Nicaragua for **Magill** and **The Sunday Tribune** and more recently worked in London with the British Nicaragua Solidarity Campaign. 'The Last of the Mohicans' is his first published creative work and he has just completed a novel for which he is hoping to find a publisher. His sister is the rock singer Sinead O'Connor.*

It was about three years since I'd seen him. And here he was, sweating behind the burger bar in Euston Station, a vision of polyester and fluorescent light. Jesus Christ. So Marion was right that time. Eddie Virago, selling double cheeseburgers for a living. I spluttered his name as he smiled in puzzled recognition over the counter. My God, Eddie Virago. In the pub he kept saying it was great to see me. Really wild he said. I should have let him know I was coming to London. This was just unreal.

Eddie was the kind of guy I tried to hang around with in college. Suave, cynical, dressed like a Sunday supplement. He'd arrive deliberately late for lectures and swan into Theatre L, permanent pout on his lips. He sat beside me one day in the first week and asked me for a light. Then he asked me for a cigarette. From then on we were friends. After pre-revolutionary France we'd sit on the middle floor of the canteen sipping coffee and avoiding Alice the tea-trolley lady. "Where did you get that tray?" she'd whine, "no trays upstairs." And Eddie would interrupt his monologue on the role of German expressionism in the development of *film noir* to remove his feet from the perilous path of her brush. "Alice's Restaurant" he called it. I didn't know what he was talking about but I laughed anyway.

He was pretty smart our Eddie. He was a good-looking bastard too. I never realised it at first, but gradually I noticed all the girls in the class wanted to get to know me. Should have known it wasn't really me they were interested in. "Who's your friend?" they'd simper, giggling like crazy. The rugby girls really liked him. You know the type. The ones who sit in the corridors calculating the cost of the lecturer's suits. All school scarves, dinner dances and summers in New York. Without a visa of course. More exciting that way. Eddie hated them all. He resisted every coy advance, every uncomfortable botched flirtation. They were bloody convent schoolgirls. All talk and no action. He said there was just one thing they needed and they weren't going to get it from him.

Professor Gough liked making risqué jokes about the nocturnal activities of Napoleon and everyone in the class was shocked. Everyone except Eddie. He'd laugh out loud and drag on his cigarette and laugh again while everybody blushed and stared at him. He said that was the trouble with Ireland. He said we were all hung up about sex. It was unhealthy. It was no wonder the mental homes were brimming over.

Eddie had lost his virginity at the age of fourteen, in a thatched cottage in Kerry. Next morning, he'd shaved with a real razor for the first time and he'd felt like a real man. As the sun dawned on his manhood he had flung his scabby old electric into the Atlantic. Then himself and his nineteen-year-old deflowerer ("deflorist" he called her) had strolled down the beach talking about poetry. She'd written to him from France a few times, but he'd never answered. It didn't do to get too involved. The entire Western Civilisation was hung up on possession Eddie said. People had to live their own lives and get away from guilt-trips.

We were close, Eddie and me. I bought him drinks and cigarettes and he let me stay in his place when I was kicked out that time. His parents gave him the money to live in a flat in Donnybrook. He called them his "old dears". I went home after a while but I never forgot my two weeks on the southside with Eddie. We stayed up late looking at films and listening to The Doors and The Jesus and Mary Chain and talking about sex a lot. Eddie like to talk about sex a lot. He said I didn't know what was ahead of me. He was amazed that I hadn't done it. Absolutely amazed. He envied me actually, because if he had it all to do over again, the first time was definitely the best. But that was Catholic Ireland. We were all repressed, and we had to escape. James Joyce was right. Snot green sea, what a line. It wasn't the same in India he said. Sex was divine to them. They had their priorities right.

Eddie went away that summer, to Germany, and he came back with a gaggle of new friends. They were all in Trinity, and they'd worked in the same gherkin factory as him. They were big into drugs and funny hair-cuts and Ford Fiestas. Eddie had the back and sides of his head shaved and he let his fringe grow down over his eyes and dyed it. Alice the tea-trolley lady would cackle at him in the canteen. "Would you look?" she'd scoff. "The Last of the Mohicans." Everyone laughed but Eddie didn't care. He didn't even blush. He rubbed glue and toothpaste into his quiff to make it stand up and even in the middle of the most crowded room, you could always tell where Eddie was. His orange hair bobbed on a sea of short back and sides.

He went to parties in his new friends' houses, and they all slept with each other. No strings attached. No questions asked. He brought me to one of them once, in a big house in Dalkey. Lots of glass everywhere. That's all I remember. Lots of glass. And paintings on the walls, by Louis le Brocquy and that other guy who's always painting his penis. You know the one. That was where I met Marion. She was in the kitchen searching the fridge while two philosophy students groped under the table. She didn't like these parties much. We sat in the garden eating cheese sandwiches and drinking beer. Eddie stumbled out and asked me if I wanted a joint. I said no. I wasn't in the mood. Marion got up to leave, with some bloke in a purple shirt who was muttering about deconstruction. Eddie said he wouldn't know the meaning of the word.

We bumped into her again at a gig in The Underground one Sunday night. It turned out the deconstructionist was her brother and he was in the band. When she asked me what I thought I said they were pretty interesting. She thought they were terrible. I bought her a drink and she asked me back to her place in Rathmines. In the jacks I whispered to Eddie that I didn't want him tagging along. He said he got the picture. Standing on the corner of Stephen's Green he winked at us and said "Goodnight young lovers, and if you can't be good be careful."

It wasn't at all like Eddie said it would be. Afterwards I laughed when she asked me had it been my first time. Was she kidding? I'd lost it in a cottage in Kerry when I was fourteen. She smiled and said yes, she'd only been kidding. All night long I tossed and turned in her single bed listening to the police cars outside. I couldn't wait to tell Eddie about it. We went for breakfast in Bewleys the next morning. Me and Marion I mean. She looked different without make-up. I felt embarrassed as she walked around the flat in tights and underwear. It was months later that I admitted I'd been lying about my sexual experience. She laughed and said she'd known all along. She said I paid too much attention to Eddie. That was our first row. She said that for someone who wasn't hung up he sure talked a lot of bullshit about it.

At first Eddie was alright about Marion and me. I told him we had done it and he clapped me on the back and asked me how it was. I said I knew what he'd been talking about. It had been unreal. He nodded wisely and asked me something about positions. I said I had to go to a lecture.

But as I started spending more time with Marion he got more sarcastic. He started asking me how was the little woman, and what was it like to be happily married. He got a big kick out of it and it made me squirm. He'd introduce me to another of his endless friends. "This is Johnny," he'd say, "he's strictly monogamous." We still went for coffee after lectures, but I was more and more alone in the company of Eddie and his disciples. Marion took me to anti-amendment meetings and Eddie said I was wasting my time. He said it didn't make any difference. Irish people took their direction from the Catholic Church. "You haven't a hope," he laughed. "Abortion? Jesus Christ, we're not even ready for contraception." I tried to tell him it wasn't just about abortion but he scoffed and said he'd heard it all before.

Eddie dropped out a few months before our finals. He left a note on my locker saying he'd had enough. He was going to London to get into film. Writing mainly, but he hoped to direct of course, in the end. London was where the action was. He was sick and tired of this place anyway. It was nothing. A glorified tax haven for rich tourists and pop stars. A cultural backwater that time forgot. He said no one who ever did anything stayed in Ireland. You had to get out to be recognised.

I was sad to see him go, specially because he couldn't even tell me to my face. But in a way it was a relief. Me and Eddie, we'd grown far apart. It wasn't that I didn't like him exactly. I just knew that secretly we embarrassed the hell out of each other. So I screwed his note into a ball and went off to the library. And as I sat staring out the window at the lake and the concrete, I tried my best to forget all about him.

Marion broke it off with me the week before the exams started. She said no hard feelings but she reckoned we'd run our course. I congratulated her on her timing. We were walking through Stephen's Green, and the children were bursting balloons and hiding behind the statues. She said she just didn't know where we were going anymore. I said I didn't know about her, but I was going to Madigan's. She said that was the kind of thing Eddie would have said. And I felt really good about that. She kissed me on the cheek, said sorry and sloped off down Grafton Street. I felt the way you do when the phone's just been slammed down on you. I thought if one of those Hare Krishnas comes near me I'll kick his head in.

I got a letter from Eddie once. Just once. He said he was getting on fine, but it was taking a while to meet the right people. Still, he was glad he'd escaped "the stifling provincialism" and he regretted nothing. He was having a wild time and there was so much to do in London. Party City. And the women! Talk about easy. I never got round to answering him. Well, I was still pretty upset about Marion for a while, and then there was all that hassle at home. I told them I'd be only too happy to get out and look for a job if there were any jobs to look for. My father said that was fine talk, and that the trouble with me was that they'd been too bloody soft on me. He'd obviously wasted his time, subsidising my idleness up in that place that was supposedly a university.

Eventually it all got too much. I moved in with Alias, into an upstairs flat on Leeson Street. My mother used to cry when I went home to do my washing on Sunday afternoons. Alias was a painter. I met him at one of Eddie's parties. The walls of the flat were plastered with paintings of naked bodies, muscles rippling, nipples like champagne corks. He said it didn't matter that they didn't look like the models. Hadn't I ever heard of imagination! I said yeah, I'd heard of it.

He was putting his portfolio together for an exhibition and living on the dole. He told everyone he had an Arts Council grant. He was alright, but he didn't have the depth of Eddie and he was a bit of a slob. He piled up his dirty clothes in the middle of his bedroom floor and he kept his empty wine bottles in the wardrobe. And the bathroom. And the kitchen. I got a job eventually, selling rubbish bags over the phone. There are thirty-seven different sizes of domestic and industrial plastic refuse sacks. I bet you didn't know that. I had to ring up factories and offices and ask them if they wanted to reorder. They never seemed to want to. I wondered what they did with all their rubbish. "Shredders," said Mr Smart. "The shredders will be my undoing." It was always hard to get the right person on the line. Mr Smart said not to fool around with secretaries, go straight for the decision-makers. They always seemed to be tied up. The pay was nearly all commission too, so I never had much cash to spare. The day I handed in my notice Mr Smart said he was disappointed in me. He thought I would have a bit more tenacity. I told him to shag off. I said sixty-five pence basic per hour didn't buy much in the way of tenacity. "Or courtesy either," he said, tearing up my reference.

That afternoon I ran into Marion on O'Connell Bridge. We went for a coffee in a small place in Abbey Street and had a bit of a laugh. I told her about chucking the job and she said I was dead right. She told me a secret. It wasn't confirmed yet, but fingers crossed. She was going off to Ethiopia. She was sick of just talking, she wanted to do something about the world. If Bob Geldof could do it, why couldn't she? I said that was great and maybe I'd do the same. Then she asked me all about Alias and the new flat and we talked about the old days. It seemed so long ago. I had almost forgotten what she looked like. She said her friend Mo had just written a postcard from London. She'd seen a guy who looked just like Eddie Virago in a burger joint in Euston Station. Except he had a short back and sides. I laughed out loud. Eddie selling hamburgers for a living? Someone of his talent? That would be the day. She said it was nice to get postcards all the same. She showed it to me. It had a guy on it with a red Mohican hair-cut. Mo said she'd bought that one because it reminded her of how Eddie used to look in the old days. She said she'd always fancied him. Marion said that she'd send me a card from Ethiopia, if they had them. She never did.

In the pub Eddie and I didn't have much to say, except that it was great to see each other. When I told him about the postcard story he said it all went to prove you couldn't trust anyone and he sipped meaningfully at his pint. After closing time we got the tube up to the West End, to a disco Eddie knew in Soho. Drunks lolled around the platforms singing and crying. The club was a tiny place, with sweat running down the walls. Eddie asked the black bouncer if Eugene was in tonight. "Who?" said the bouncer. "You know Eugene, the other doorman?" He shrugged and said "Not tonight man. I dunno no Eugene." I paid Eddie in, because it wasn't his pay day till Thursday. He was really sorry about that.

Downstairs he had to lean across the table, shaking the drinks, to shout in my ear. The writing was going alright. Of course it was all contacts, all a closed shop. He was still trying though. In fact he'd just finished a script and although he wasn't free to reveal the details he didn't mind telling me there was quite a bit of interest in it. He only hoped it wasn't too adventurous. Thatcher had the BBC by the short and curlies he said. They wouldn't take any risks at all. And Channel 4 wasn't the same since Isaacs left. Bloody shame that, man of his creative flair.

He'd made lots of friends though, in the business. I'd probably meet them later on. They only went out clubbing late at night. Nocturnal animals he said. It was more cool to do that. They were great people, really wild. Honestly, from Neil Jordan downwards the business was wonderful. Of course he'd met Jordan. He crashed at his place once after a particularly wild party. Really decent bloke. There was a good scene in London. No he didn't listen to the old bands any more. He was all into Acid House. He said that was this year's thing. Forget The Clash. Guitar groups were out. The word was acid. I said I hadn't heard any. What was it like? He said he couldn't describe it really. It wasn't the kind of music you could put into words.

I did meet one of his friends later on in the night. He saw her standing across the dance floor and beckoned her over. She mustn't have seen him. So he said he'd be back in a second and weaved through the gyrating bodies to where she was. They chatted for a few minutes and then she came over and sat down. Shirley was a model. From Dublin too. Well, trying to make it as a model. She knew Bono really well. He was a great bloke she said, really dead on. She'd known him and Ali for absolute yonks, and success hadn't changed them at all. Course she hadn't seen him since Wembley last year. Backstage. They were working on the new album. She'd heard the rough mixes and it was a real scorcher. This friend of hers played them to her. A really good friend of hers actually, who went out with your man from Hot House Flowers. The one with the hair. She kept forgetting his name. She said she was no good at all for Irish names. She really regretted it, specially since she moved over here, but she couldn't speak a word of Irish. She let us buy her a drink each. I paid for Eddie's. Then she had to run. Early start tomorrow, had to be in the studio by eight-thirty. "Ciao," she said when she went. "Ciao Eddie."

It was after four when they kicked us out. The streets of Soho were jostling with mini-cabs and hot-dog sellers. A crowd filtered out of Ronnie Scott's Club, just around the corner. Sleek black women in furs and lace. Tall men in sharp suits. Eddie apologised for his friends not showing up. He said if he'd known I was coming he would have arranged a really wild session. Next time. He knew a really great hip-hop club up in Camden Town, really wild, but in a very cool kind of way.

In the coffee bar in Leicester Square he was quiet. The old career hadn't been going exactly to plan. He was getting there all right. But much slower than he thought. Still, that was the business. Things got a bit lonely he said. He got so frustrated, so down. It was hard being an exile. He didn't want to be pretentious or anything but he knew how Sam Beckett must have felt. If he didn't believe in himself as much as he did, he didn't know how he could go on. He would have invited me back to his place only a few people were crashing there so there wasn't the room. But next time, honest. It was a big place. But still, it was always full. People were always just dropping in unannounced. "You know how it is." He laughed again as we ordered another cappuccino.

"I have measured out my life in coffee spoons," he said, as he sipped painfully. He always drank Nicaraguan actually, at home. Very into the cause. I said I knew nothing about it. He started to tell me all the facts but I said I really had to go. My aunt would be worried sick about me. If I didn't get home soon she'd call the police or something. He nodded and said fair enough. He had to split as well.

We stood in the rain on Charing Cross Road while he scribbled his address on a soggy beer mat. He told me it was good to see me again. I told him I nearly didn't recognise him with the new haircut. He'd had to get rid of that, for work. Anyway punk was dead. It was history now. "You should come over here for good," he said, "it's a great city." I shook his hand and said I'd think about it. He told me not to let the opportunity pass me by.

The taxi driver asked me where I wanted to go. He loved Ireland. The wife was half-Irish and they'd been over a few times now. Lovely country. Terrible what was going on over there though. He said they were bloody savages, bloody cowboys and Indians. No offence, but he just couldn't understand it. I said I couldn't either. In his opinion it was all to do with religion.

By the time we got to Greenwich the sun was painting the sky over the river. He said he hoped I enjoyed the rest of my holiday. I hadn't any money left to give him a tip.

*Joseph O'Connor has since become one of Ireland's best known and best-selling writers. He has published two critically acclaimed novels, **Cowboys and Indians** and **Desperadoes**, and a collection of short stories, **True Believers**, and contributes a column to **The Sunday Tribune**.*

In 1994, a collection of his comic writing, **The Secret World of the Irish Male** (New Island Books) was a massive best-seller in Ireland and has been published in the UK. His first play, **Red Roses and Petrol**, (1995) has proved to be equally successful.

1989

TELL ME

COLM O'GAORA

Colm O'Gaora was born in Dublin in 1965 and read English at UCD. He lives in London, working as a freelance journalist and writing a novel. This is his first published work. He is a son of the RTE news-reader Padraig O'Gaora.

Somehow, despite his denials, I knew that my father and I had been down this way before. A picture of the stone-walled, tree-lined road had hung like a heat-haze in my memory and had been carried forward like original sin from that one day in my childhood when I had been driven this same way by him. In those days I had believed, as all children inevitably do, that my father could do no wrong, whatever that was.

I was on my way back to London and Dad had offered to drive me to the airport. We set off ridiculously early because he had suggested that we drive up into the surrounding hills so that I could look down upon the city that I was once again leaving behind me. He has always been a true romantic, my father, and so I feigned enthusiasm in order to please him. It was indeed a vibrantly sunny day and the air hummed with high summer, which lent considerable strength to his argument. So we set off towards the hills which shimmered in the heat outside Dublin. The car brought us swiftly along beneath yawning canopies of leaves which swayed in the breeze, parting just often enough for us to catch glimpses of the city bustling on the horizon. The heat made my jeans stick to the vinyl car seat and I fidgeted around

47

trying to free myself. Dad didn't notice my discomfort and I put this down to him concentrating on the winding roads we travelled along. I wound the window the whole way down and let the rush of air whip beads of sweat off my forehead, being careful to dodge the flailing roadside briars. Now I was glad that he had brought me up here before I left. Here was something I could not do so easily in my adopted home-town and I found the experience exhilarating.

Then we turned into a road where the stone walls were higher and more solid and where trees grew regularly along the roadside entwining overhead to block out much of the sunlight. I turned to look back at the receding city but what glimpses I had had before were now blocked by the closely grown trees. Looking at my father for reassurance I saw his expression change from one of amused abandon to a bewildered almost lost expression that spread across his features and seeped into the air itself. My childhood memory slithered back to me.

"We've been this way before, haven't we, Dad?" I said looking at him.

"No, well I don't think so," he replied, "it's very different from the rest of the countryside though, isn't it? Very peaceful and still and not so stiflingly hot as the rest. It's the trees that do it."

We continued on down the road for another two-hundred yards or so, Dad almost letting the car roll the distance. We turned left into a similar road which was, however, only half the width of the previous one and blackberry bushes pushed against the side of the car as we progressed slowly along it. The road surface was broken by tufts of grass and the tyres crushed the shattered remains of egg shells lying on the road under the trees.

"Are you sure you aren't lost, Dad?" I asked, "it looks as if no-one has been here for ages."

"Don't worry, son, I knew where I was going."

His head turned slowly from side to side as if looking for an exit at the side of the road although the obvious way to go seemed to be to follow the road on down the hill or to reverse back to the wider road we had left behind.

"Ah! I knew it was along here somewhere," he said, slipping the car into reverse and turning to look between the headrests as we inched back along the way we had come.

A rusting water-pump lurked moss-ridden in the tangle of vegetation at the roadside. As he reversed, his forearm rested upon my shoulder for a moment. He was trembling almost imperceptibly. Then he brought the car to a halt. I peered across him to see what we had stopped at. It was an iron gate, overrun with bindweed which rendered it all but invisible to anyone who wasn't looking for it.

"You must have been here before," I said as I turned to undo my seatbelt, "how could you have found this unless you knew where to look for it?"

He didn't appear to have heard me and was already getting out of the car. He stepped over to the gate and I noticed that it was well-made and not at all typical of the grid-iron gate so common in the countryside. Tearing the bindweed away from the latch he lifted it slightly and pushed the gate. It swung inwards with the shrillest of squeaks and he turned to face me with a look of anticipation on his face. He was bemused that I hadn't moved from the car.

"Where's this?" I asked.

"Come on, don't look so worried," he said. "Here, you can drive the car in, or have you forgotten all I taught you?"

He turned and walked back in between the gateposts and I followed him tentatively in the car. He pushed the gate shut behind me. I parked the car beside a wild and bushy privet hedge and as I stepped out I noticed that although the ground was covered in grass, it had once been a gravel driveway.

"Come on, we don't have much time to hang around," he said disappearing through a gap in the hedge cleverly disguised by its wild branches.

I stood quite still once on the other side of the hedge. Before me was a bedraggled two-storey house overgrown with clematis and honeysuckle. The humming air was heavy with their scent and bumble-bees hovered around the building, visiting the plethora of blooms that exploded across the walls and windows. Paint peeled in eloquent long strips off the front door, but the glass in the windows seemed quite intact, and despite the enveloping shrubbery the house appeared to be in good condition. Around it the garden was a teeming mass of trailing flowers and attendant insects. The grass was knee-deep and bent like an angler's rod with the weight of ripening seeds.

Dad sneezed violently. The air, thick with pollen, had worked its way into the membranes of his sinuses and he put the back of his hand to his nose and sniffled loudly.

"Yes son, you were here once before, when you must have been only five or six years old. I was much younger too and the garden was neat and tidy, and that peeling door marine blue. I know because I painted it for her."

He was looking the house up and down with his arms folded as he said this, rocking back and forwards off the ball of his foot. In his fist he held a large key attached to a leather key-ring I had not seen before. Then I sneezed too.

Opening the door with the key he allowed me in before him. Sunlight streamed into the room through two bay windows at the rear although the matrix of branches that criss-crossed the glass made the shadows appear like the stained glass windows in Saint Patrick's Cathedral. Dust danced in the brilliant shafts of light, the tiny particles assuming their own inner harmony and seeming to exist on individual planes of movement since they never appeared to collide with one another. I was momentarily mesmerised. To my right a stairs led upwards to a landing. At the

foot of the stairs was an open doorway into a tiled kitchen. A
solitary bowl sat in the middle of the table and two bare but solid
chairs stood in expectant silence. A butterfly flitted through the
beams of light filtering into the kitchen, alighting first on the
table's edge and eventually coming to rest on the lone light bulb
suspended from the ceiling. In the alcove beneath the stairs a
rocking chair upholstered in deepest burgundy sat awaiting new
momentum. I wondered how long it had waited.

I would have expected an abandoned place like this to smell
of staleness, but instead the air was palely tinged with the scent
of honeysuckle from the plants outside. This lent a further sense
of unreality to the house, almost as if time had stood still here
since the last occupant had left.

Dad stood at the bay window towards the back of the house.
The sunlight streamed in upon him creating a halo effect amongst
the thinning hairs on his head. I joined him there, he like a lizard
soaking up the rays and the memories and I like the devious
schoolchild filled with wonder at having fallen upon a secret
place. Only this was not just a secret place to be, it was also a
secret place in the mists of my father's mind and I was beginning
to feel like an unwelcome intruder, even though he had brought
me here. He laid a heavy hand on my shoulder and turned slowly
back into the room. There was no need for him to say anything
now, and no need for me to ask.

How many times had he stood here in the evenings with her
in his arms, his hands across her tummy, her shoulders drawn up
like a squirming cat? Had he read to her from Keats as he used
to do for my mother, or had they sat mutely on the window box
enjoying each other's silent company? Had they laughed at each
other's foibles or the paleness of their fair skins while they
undressed each other in swimming moonlight? I needed no
answers. All was etched into the character of the house and into
the expressions drifting like clouds across his face.

Leaning forward, I unlatched and pushed carefully one of the
windows in front of me. Fragile blisters of crackling varnish

scattered to the ground. Warm air rushed quietly in, like a baby breathing its last on the delivery-room table. I shut the window suddenly, raising dust from the sill. Outside a violent gust of wind rushed through the bowing tree-tops, startling the humming insects in its haste.

"Dad," I called, "don't forget the time."

Nothing answered but the creaking of the upstairs floorboards in response to his weight. I went up to join him.

Upstairs was a warren of small rooms. The doors swung easily inwards, thin layers of dust floating off their oaken panels and onto the floor as we entered each room in turn. In the study a sheaf of papers lay on the corner of the writing desk. I recognised his familiar script in the blue fountain pen he preferred but I did not dare read the carefully written words. An oil lamp stood in the corner, its blackened wick turning inwards upon itself in its desiccated afterlife.

At the bedroom I hesitated. Dad stood by the dresser running his finger along the top edge of the mirror and letting the dust slide down in small clumps and come to rest on the lace cloth that covered the space where her make-up and powder-puff would have lain. The room was bright and airy although spiders had obviously colonised a corner of it at one time. Their destitute webs hung drape-like from the covings and swayed in time to our body movements. The large bed was still made. A deep red over-blanket had been bleached a sickly yellow on one side by the sun and as he patted it dust rose in plumes from its surface, like an old man breathing his last. He must have lain many times upon this bed, fixing his gaze upon the ceiling or maybe upon her damp down-covered skin after they had made love together one more time before he returned home to his wife and my mother. I glanced at him.

"Sorry," he murmured.

As I looked at him bowed over the bed, strands of long hair slid forwards off his head and hung like the spiders' drapes about his face. He appeared to be a mourner crouched in intense concentration over an ebbing corpse as if willing life into what lay before him, memories waxing and waning, tears pouring into the warm heart of the day. She was still there, in his conscience at least, if not elsewhere. Was coming back like this a last attempt to unthread himself from the undertows her departure caused in the submarine seas of his life? Or maybe a last chance to immerse himself in a warm ocean of memories, or perhaps to engage in the internal sea music of the soul.

"Dad, come on. Let's go, there's no more time."

"There isn't really, is there? Time for nothing but regret in the end. Yeah, let's go. It's better to leave this place now."

At the bottom of the stairs he paused and I brushed past him. When I reached the door I turned to see where he was. He stood half-hidden in the shadow of the open door of a tall closet. His hand clenched its handle so hard that the blood ran away from his knuckles and into his fingers and the back of his hand. The knuckles shone white in the gloom. As he drew away from the darkness I saw the dress draped over his forearm. It was a riot of colour in the pall of shadows at the foot of the stairs. The collar was vibrant peach and an explosion of blossoms ran from it down to the hem. Few would find it particularly attractive.

He ran a finger along its smooth yielding length, little ripples bouncing in front of his finger as it went, ending in a flick and swish of material at the bottom. The dress swung silently like a pendulum weighing time before coming to a halt.

"It was always her favourite dress," he said in a shaky voice and stepped into the centre of the room.

From his pocket he drew the brass cigarette lighter Mum had bought him for his birthday two years ago.

Carefully he unscrewed the reservoir cap at the end and allowed drops of clear lighter fuel to gather and swell before they dropped onto the colourful fabric of the dress. The drips became a trickle shortly before he tightened the cap, stifling the flow.

Hanging the dress at arms' length he lit the hem. Blue flames broke in a smile across the blossoms. While he draped the dress over the rocking chair I opened the door.

He didn't look back until we had turned the corner onto the wider road. A pall of smoke rose from a gap amongst the trees before being whisked up and dispersed by the breeze that blew across the side of the hill. I wound down the window and could barely hear the crackling of the flames. The sound of departing insects grew to a cacophony in my ears, and I turned back to my father. I caught the trailing edge of that last cloud drifting across his face. His eyes were once again on the road.

"Tell me," I said.

And he did.

*Colm O'Gaora has since published an acclaimed debut collection of stories, **Giving Ground** (Cape, 1993) and is currently completing a novel.*

1989

LOVE IN HISTORY

EOIN McNAMEE

*Eoin McNamee was born in Kilkeel, Co Down in 1961. His poetry and prose have been widely published in Ireland. A selection of his work appeared in **Raven Introductions 5**, and 'Love in History' is included in his fiction debut, **The Last of Deeds** which is just published by Raven Arts Press.*

Sergeant Gabriel Hooper had a Kodak monochrome photograph of Betty Grable on the wall of his room. In the photograph she was sitting astride the barrel of an anti-aircraft gun. Her skin was white and her black lips were drawn back from her teeth in a smile which captured the light of an entire aircraft carrier.

If you pulled down the top of Betty Grable's swimming costume the breasts underneath would be white, shaved cones like pencils with exact graphite tips.

In 1945 the uniform crotches of USAAF pilots were stiff with beauty.

Sergeant Gabriel Hooper had been stationed in RAF Cranfield since 1942. His billet was in an old house beside the seven salty miles of the runway. Sand blown up from the beach piled against the seaweed gable wall. New hangars creaked in derelict breezes, and the red singing tongue of a windsock pointed towards Russian Winters and Tripoli landings.

At night he sat on his bed in USAAF shorts and singlet writing letters to his wife in handwriting which seemed like some complicated calculation of cross-winds and velocity over target. Somewhere in Kansas or Oklahoma was a dusty mailbox crammed with letters which his wife never answered.

In the bedroom of 1945 Adelene fastened the catch of her brassiere around her waist and twisted its stiff points upwards and around to put it into place. With a sweater over the top her breasts were like the tops of pencils, her black hair was a replica of lacquer, her white thighs stormed the map of the heart.

During the day Adelene counted cellophane packets of American stockings and ate American peaches from the tin with her fingers. At night pilots held her against the perimeter fence, flattening her breasts against their tunic pockets. When she took a job in the aerodrome canteen she adjusted her mouth with lipstick using the polished tea-urn as a mirror in which pilots returning from missions looked for her mouth, lurid with desire or grief.

When Gabriel Hooper saw her there for the first time he thought of Betty Grable. Then he thought of his wife's kiss, the light, sour touch of her lips like sweat drying between the shoulder-blades. He looked down at his blue-veined hands and they trembled like the ancient stained-glass of cathedrals in Dresden or Coventry.

Gabriel Hooper kept a photograph of himself and his wife in his breast pocket. The pocket of a dead pilot is often found to contain a rabbit's foot, or photo-booth snapshot from a port entrance or railway station or other point of departure.

In the photograph Gabriel Hooper was sitting in a deckchair. Behind him was a water tower and beyond that grass stretched towards a monotone skyline. His wife sat between his legs, looking into the sun, expressionless as a woman of Europe, deprived of time and place to mourn.

Each Saturday night a truck left the airfield for the town. The truck brought aircrews to the Aurora cinema, or the Central ballroom, or the Island café. Tonight Gabriel Hooper was sitting

under the canvas flaps beside the tailgate where he could see
bombers practising night-landings at the far end of the runway,
the red flares of their exhausts like islands burning in a smoky
archipelago across the Pacific.

Adelene heard the bombers from her bedroom. She looked
into the mirror with the brown tip of a hairpin between her lips
and thought about the incendiary sky over Dresden terrible with
white pearls of men's flesh.

When the truck pulled up outside the Central ballroom the
street was busy with men in uniform, their pockets full of Fanny
Mae's toffees, razor blades and silk stockings. They were
watched ravenously from windows and mirrors by thousands of
women with red lips and starved fox-fur collars.

Beside the glass box-office of the Aurora cinema was a
full-length poster of Betty Grable. On the steps of the Central
ballroom two military policemen beat a black serviceman with
batons. When he looked up his mouth was a red rose.

Inside the ballroom Gabriel Hooper watched Adelene dance
in arms that smelt of Palmolive. Gabriel Hooper watched her
with such intensity that his eyes could have pierced
immeasurable distances of war and desolation to reach the exact
spot under the left breast where Betty Grable's monochrome
heart pumped Pearl Harbour, or Omaha Beach through paper
veins. He drew a Lucky Strike from the packet and tapped
unanswerable signals with the tip of the cigarette on the lid of
the packet.

She watched him approach in the mirrored lid of a powder
compact. When he asked her to dance she answered yes and he
smiled the wide, blue smile of a drought in the cornbelt.

I never seen you before, she said, close to his ear. I never
noticed you in the canteen. I never seen you drunk like the others.
I never seen you playing baseball behind the hangars, or dancing
like a flag in white USAAF shorts with the other men when they

swim on the beach, standing waistdeep in the water or floating on their backs smoking, like Daily Mail photographs of endless husbands floating in the shallow, oily waters of Dunkirk.

I've seen you before, he said. I've seen your red lips in the canteen after a late shift as I lay awake and alone. I've heard you laugh with men as I lay alone when the sound of a wife's kiss is the sound of Betty Grable's heart broken with frost in the night.

Fancy a drink? she said, I'm parched. They went to the balcony. He fetched two cups of tea. Do you miss home? she asked. Are you homesick?

How many in your family? Are you married? He held out the photograph of his wife and himself mutely, as if they were the victims of an accident, without mentioning dates of birth, or the name of a town in Kansas or Oklahoma. Lovely, Adelene said, is that you?

When Adelene went to the toilet Gabriel Hooper looked again at his own face and his wife's face, dazzled by sunlight on zinc barns, and rainless seasons of drought and dustbowl politics. He lowered the tip of his cigarette to his wife's face and inhaled the moist, chemical smell of burnt Kodak.

Outside she slipped her arm through his. They walked out of town until they reached the perimeter fence of the aerodrome. What's your wife's name? she asked. Cissy, he said. It was the sound that sand from the beach made when the wind carried it across concrete.

Do you think I look like Betty Grable? she asked, they say I'm the dead spit of her. Wait till you see.

She put her back against one of the fence posts and raised her face so that her throat was visible, and he could see, like the faces of an audience, white porcelain insulators on telegraph poles.

Have you got a rabbit's foot? she asked. He nodded. Where? He touched the outside of his trouser pocket lightly. Her hand travelled past a handkerchief, a stub of pencil, coins and a brass Zippo to the shreds of tobacco in the pocket lining where there was a soft foot the size of a lost button and he smiled at the memory of a rabbit surprised in the open on the yellow grass of Kansas or Oklahoma.

Gabriel Hooper woke at dawn and walked naked to the window. In the distance rain scratched the tin roofs of Nissan huts and hangars. Driven inland by an advancing frontal system seagulls squatted at the edge of the wet, black runway. Behind him Adelene turned in her sleep and the sheets crackled like parachute silk drifting over cornfield or open sea.

A wife's name is the sound that sand makes when the wind carries it across concrete. A wife's kiss is the sound of Betty Grable's heart broken with frost in the night. Gabriel Hooper walked naked to the window to look for America but it was lost in an advancing frontal system, weather in which men find themselves mapless and bereft.

If you pull down the top of Betty Grable's swimming costume her breasts are as smooth as the cone of a navigator's unreliable pencil. If you pull down the top of her swimming costume her breasts accuse and her navel is like a spotlight scanning the skyline of Europe for love in history, finding you then losing you between gaps in the clouds.

*The Last of Deeds was short-listed for The Irish Times/Aer Lingus Irish Fiction Prize, and was republished by Penguin to include a much extended version of 'Love in History'. In 1994 his first full-length novel, **Resurrection Man**, was published to massive critical acclaim by Picador, and is about to be published in America, France, Italy and Denmark. His debut collection of poems, **The Language of Birds**, was published by New Island Books in 1995.*

1990

TRESSES

COLUM McCANN

*Colum McCann was born in 1965 and is a graduate of the College of Journalism in Rathmines. He worked for two years in the **Evening Press** and was named 'Young Journalist of the Year'. He has spent the last three years in the United States, where he bicycled from coast to coast and worked at a number of jobs including mechanic, ranch hand, taxi driver, fisherman, fire-fighter, waiter and freelance writer. He is currently teaching delinquent teen-agers at Miracle Farm in Colorado. This is his first published fiction.*

For many weeks now they have slept like spoons, back to front, cold from the toes up, these young lovers.

Her pale body — too old for its curves, too young for its fruit — is curled along the hot-roof brown of his. She has blonde Rapunzel hair that lies chaotic across his face, almost obscuring a Confederate-flag bandanna that he stretches over his head. He hasn't changed the bandanna for eight days now.

The stars of the defeated are ringed with the salt of sweat, and stray pieces of tar, from the building site, stick to the bedsheets. Her small naked chest floats against his dirty T-shirt, her stomach is neat in the small of his back and her knees begin their bend at his thighs.

Grainne does not like the way things have changed.

As they sleep, in a motel room that has become their home, a seaside wind, shore-side America, soft with hope, song of freshness, slides through their bedroom window. The breeze dances along the cheap carpet, towards the overturned ashtray at the foot of the bed, the well-smoked butts making a map of accusation. Here. There. Yellowed newspapers — the *Connaught Telegraph* and the *Mayo News* — lie scattered on the floor, sent, like the fresh wind, all the way across the sea. A milk carton on the floor shows photos of missing children. There's a Zippo lighter, a pair of Ray-bans and crumpled cans of beer. A Hohner harmonica waits for the blues.

In the bathroom, beyond the bedroom, there are hairs clogged in the sink and a puddle of puke on the floor. A tube of blue lipstick, left from a party three nights before, sits on top of the cabinet. On the wall there is some Trinity graffiti scrawled with mascara: "Keep Cape Cod beautiful. Buy a beer. Blow a bong. Bonk a blond. Burn a billboard." With a different colour mascara, signed by a UCD student, there are the words *"Beidh an bua againn"*. When Grainne saw it, a couple of days ago, she recognised the words of the dead hunger-striker and wondered what victory they referred to — the bonking of a blond or the burning of a billboard or the sweet blow of marijuana? History and youth kicking words around —

The morning wind ruffles the yachts painted on the shower curtain. Sometimes, when she is on her own in the motel room, Grainne puts a sea-shell ashtray to the drawings and she swears to herself that she can hear the laughter of the harbour-rich bellowing down and spitting upon her naked poverty.

The wind, the wind, the wind, stale after its visit, bounces off a cracked mirror, retreats out of the second-floor room, as if scared, with backward eyes, and darts out through a hole in the curtain. Later it will bring with it the halitosis of heat.

And as the wind dies, Grainne, the back spoon, the young lover, stirs, awakens with a start and touches her stomach where the child grows...

Jesus Christ, girl. Another day. Every morning I wake up and tomorrow's already here. What a life.

I keep waiting for the knock on the door and they'll be here — immigration badges and thirty-two shining white teeth, the government car under the balcony out there. They'll send us up to Boston for the big bird home. Jesus, it's scary. Fergus should never have put that brass knocker with the pig's head on the door. Oh, yeah, he thought it was very funny alright — when they come knocking they'll know they're pigs, he said, ha ha ha. And he spent ten dollars on it. Like we were made of money or something. Just so when the lads come around they can have a laugh. Knock the pigs' heads in, ha ha ha.

It won't be so funny when the real knock, knock, knock comes. I knew we should have got visas, but, no, no, he said, we'll be cool, don't worry about it, they'll never catch us, we'll use telephone numbers for our social security cards, that's the lark.

It's crazy. Living like this. Waiting like this. No green card. All red lights.

God, he smells this morning. On the piss again last night, no doubt. Pay day. All he does is rent the beer — then he pukes it out on the floor. I shouldn't even stay here. God, what a mess. It's a year and two months now, to the very day. Always said I was going to go back home, back to university. Now — Jesus — now it's different with you inside me. What if they sent me home? If my parents found out...oh, Jesus. My father would die. That knock, knock, knock — it haunts me. I can't go back. I can't, ever. Fergus doesn't even want to know.

All I want him to do is touch me like he used to. I want him to hold my belly and tell me that everything's going to be alright, that we'll rent a little wooden house down by the beach, that we'll skip on the sand and watch for dolphins and hang onto their fins. That we'll drink white wine and watch the ballerina moon dance across the ecliptic.

Oh Jesus. Gotta get up. I don't ever want to get out of bed. Don't make me sick again this morning, please. It's bad enough having to clean up his puke, but this morning sickness ... Anyway. God. Gotta get up. Cheeseburgers to be flipped down in paradise...

She pulls on Fergus' Waterboys T-shirt that falls, like her mermaid hair, to her knees. Opening the door of the room out to the balcony she can feel the blast of morning freshness in her eyes, sea-blue and watery.

She touches her stomach, scared that soon her body won't go out and around in the right places any more, and then she places both hands on the iron railings and bends over as if she is about to child-somersault back to the uncomplicated days. It's a twenty-foot drop down, but she reckons that if she clipped her toes to the railing and fell completely backwards her hair could knot a rope upon which her prince could climb, if, of course, he stood on the back of his white horse.

"Mount Parnassus," she chuckles, to nobody but herself. "What if my prince is an immigration officer in disguise?"

With the freckles of dawn still in the sky, she looks out at the quiet streets of Hyannis, a seaside town manured with bits and pieces of teenage innocence. A faint fog horn comes in from the harbour, where the yachts point their sails to Martha's Vineyard.

Nobody stirs in the rest of the motel. Quietly, greyly, the paint peels. None of the other Irish students have jobs that get them up early, apart from Eoin, who cranks his Honda at four every morning to drive all the way to Brewster, where he rakes the bunkers at the golf course, then comes home every evening and — just like Fergus — drinks himself to oblivion in the 19th Hole Bar. Next up would be Barbara, chambermaid extraordinaire, fingernail polish worn like an autograph, leaving her little hovel arm-in-arm with her latest American beau. Then there's Brendan — always late, a piece of toast in his mouth, rushing out on his bicycle to go landscaping, a big smile and wave to her up here on the balcony. Then next would be that shy girl at the end, the quiet one, with the robin redbreast smile and nasturtiums outside the —

"CARNIVAL TIME!"

Suddenly the world swoops below her and the tarmac shimmers and her legs dangle over the side of the iron railings. It takes her a moment to realise that it's Fergus who's holding her, suspended, above a violent world, above swinging blackness, by the ankles.

"Jesus Christ, Fergus, let me up!"

"Don't think I'd drop ya now, do ya?"

"Fergus, let me up!"

"Think I'd drop ya?"

"Fergus, my stomach, the..."

"Jesus H, only having a bit of fun," he says as his grip on her ankles tightens. She feels like a feather-puppet as he pulls her back over the side of the railings, her hair thrown in chaos and fright across her eyes. She grips her stomach and watches his knuckles tighten. The tar creases across his fingers. She reaches her hand out to touch his face.

"Please. Don't ever, ever do that when you know..."

But already he has gone back inside, gazing into the bathroom mirror, a cigarette lit like a decrepit James Dean, wearing a flag on his head that he doesn't understand, muttering over and over again that he's had enough, had enough, enough, enough, enough, no fun anymore, every morning's the bleedin' same. Jesus H, enough, enough, enough. He lays a sheet of newspaper — the obituary page of the *Mayo News* — over the vomit on the floor. Grainne steps back inside and sits on the edge of the rumpled bed, her head in her hands, insides peeling like the motel paint, her bare toes nudging the spilt ashtray and the ash making a map on her toes.

I'm sorry girl, I'm sorry. I hope he didn't hurt you. He doesn't mean it. He was just playing. He was just holding my ankles. He wouldn't have — He just — God, this place is a mess. I'll clean it when I get home from work. He didn't mean it, honestly. I wish the sea would roll up here. The dolphins.

They'd take us. They really would — nobody would ever hurt you...

Grainne watches him as he steps out of the bathroom, half his face covered with shaving cream, paisley boxers on, his bandanna askew. For a moment she remembers that they used to go down to the beach with a blanket, late at night, Scorpio stinging the summer sky and listen to the whistle of the waves, talk about the dolphins, play the harmonica and wrap each other in her hair. Those were the days when there wasn't a broken clock ticking away, inside her ivory tower, her embryo tower, suffocating days into weeks.

"I'm sick and tired of it," he says, standing in the bathroom doorway. She touches another cigarette butt with her toe. "I'm tired of everything. Christ, Grainne, if I had lifted you up and dangled you off the balcony three months ago you would have laughed. It's like you're a housewife now or something. I — I don't want you to have it. There's no life here for it. There's no life there. They'd call it a bastard. Why do we have to do this every morning? Every goddamn morning. You always cry. We can go to Boston, Grainne, please." He picks the Ray-bans off the floor, twirls the cord around his fingers and puts them on. "Listen, there's clinics up there. Jesus H, Grainne. You mope around. You don't smile any more. Listen to me, for crissake."

"Heard it before." She makes a labyrinth with the butts.

"I remember when you used to talk about that film course in Dublin like it was all that was important in your life. For feck sake. We'll get the money. You're nineteen years-old. It's not as if life is over or anything. All the lads keep asking me what's wrong with ya. What the hell am I supposed to say, huh?"

"You left your cigarette burning on the sink," says Grainne. "It'll fall and burn the lino."

"To hell with the lino. Talk to me."

"Where were you last night?"

"Jesus, Grainne. We were down the Duck, alright? You knew where I'd be. Besides, there was a fight. Pat Flaherty got his front teeth knocked out."

"Who?"

"Pat. The bloke who drives the taxi. Some big Yank hit him in the teeth and there was a big — Grainne, listen. I don't want to talk about it. What's the story? Boston. Yes or no?"

Silence. She watches him as his head slumps against the doorway, his curls sticking out from underneath the bandanna. He looks years older than he did yesterday. The silence sings a silkworm tune, spinning out its bowels and consuming itself until a dull thud startles her and his fist hammers against the door. He steps over to the cupboard, a tangle of summer clothes, and reaches in for a coathanger. Twisting it backwards and forwards the hanger snaps and he straightens out the curves until it is just one long piece of thin metal. Then he sucks the blood from his knuckles.

"I'm tired of it, I'm tired of it," he repeats, stepping forward, holding the hanger like a branding iron for her body, hiding his eyes behind the sunglasses. "Tired, tired, tired. Why don't you go? It'll only take a day. Nobody need know. I'll even go with you. It doesn't cost a lot of money. There are lots of clinics. Jesus, Grainne. We'd be alright then. Listen, Grainne, film producers don't have babies and flip hamburgers."

"And nuclear physicists don't get tar on their fingernails."

"Awww, dig, dig. Yes or no?" he asks. "Boston?"

She doesn't reply. She can feel an ache in her stomach, like a long-forgotten call. She reaches for her jeans and sandals, takes a look at him, standing angry in front of her, the coathanger in his hand and she begins to dress.

"Talk to me, for Christ's sake, talk to me. I'll phone today if you want me to. I'll make an appointment."

"Who wrote on the bathroom wall?"

"Shut up. Yes or no?"

Dressed, she stands up and then bends over to the ground. Her hair falls to the floor and she brushes it with sweet, smooth strokes. Bringing her head up, she pulls the hair from off her shoulders, rubs her fingers down behind her neck, looks him straight in the eyes — sure that she can see dolphins — and says: "Who are you to tiptoe on my dreamworld?"

"Who are you to tiptoe on my dreamworld, who're you to tiptoe on my dreamworld," he taunts, "who're you, very goddamn poetic, Grainne, but it doesn't mean a damn thing, who'reyou, who'reyoutotiptoe, lalalalala."

"I'm going to work."

"Go to work, then. Here, take this with you." He throws the coat-hanger at her feet. "Use it. Very effective, you know. One quick prong and it's all over. A natural abortion. Take it. Scrape it out. Tiptoe on your dreamworld. I'm sick and tired of your bullshit."

Grainne picks the coat-hanger from the floor, places it gently on the bedside table beside the photograph of her father bringing in seaweed from the Louisburgh strand, and leaves, walking down towards the harbour.

He wants me to hang you on a coat-hanger. Leave you there dangling like an absurd question mark.

God, the sea is so pretty.

Look, girl, look way out there and we might see the dolphins, out there, past the yachts. They could carry us all the way across the ocean and we'd be home. Daddy used to say that if I went to America that I'd be in Tir na nOg, the Land of Eternal Youth. But he never said anything to me about getting off the white horse and growing old. He didn't say anything about the knock, knock, knock or the things that grow inside. He said I'd be the girl that Gatsby would ache for, the Donnelly dreamchild, that I would articulate the dream.

You know, I think of strange things. I think of the big black hearse that I used to see on the streets of Louisburgh before I came over here. On Sunday mornings, on the way to Mass, the hearse always used to look bigger to me than it actually was. The old men would shuffle across the street, on their way to Gaffney's, heads bent in the wind and rain, and they'd hurry past the car, look at it, like it was a signpost or something. Like the bumper was pointing to the day when they'd be dropped down in that wooden overcoat.

Sometimes I think I see that black hearse out there, when I go into work, under the flutter of the Star Spangled Banner, up the road from the crazy golf course, and I think it's waiting here for me. And you. Sometimes now I wonder what the purpose of my flesh is — to feed life or to feed death? All these questions. Questions the questions, Daddy used to say.

Look, look, if you try real hard you can see the dolphins.

She doesn't go to work. Instead she walks along the harbour, wisps of waves at her sandals, down the unreal cleanliness of the streets of Hyannis, back to the motel. Nobody is around and she sits on the opposite balcony, lotus-legged, waiting for Fergus to leave. It takes an hour before the familiar bandanna bounces down the steps and gets into a cracked-dashboard Plymouth.

She walks, with her hair hung over her eyes, back to the motel room. She flips the pig's head door knocker and turns the key in the door. Frightened child, she hunches in the corner, cradling her stomach, a scissors in one hand, the coat-hanger in the other. Her tresses make a mask. She holds the harmonica between her teeth and sucks in hard on the heavy air. Her teeth cut into the metal. The music wails in the silence of the room. Every now and then the air conditioner kicks in. It dries the beads of sweat on her face. Harmonica. Harmonica. Harmonica. Sweat. Coat-hanger. Dolphins. Scissors. Coat-hanger. Dolphins.

It's okay, girl, it's okay. Daddy said that Gatsby would ache.

When the evening spits its orange eloquence on Hyannis, a toothless taxi driver pulls up underneath a motel room balcony. He beeps his horn. A young girl jumps down the steps and opens the back door of the car.

"You're Grainne, right? Fergus' girlfriend."

"Yeah, listen, I need to find him. Can we go around all the pubs? It's real important."

"No problem. Fergus said you looked like a mermaid. I thought you had long hair."

"I did. I left it on a coat-hanger — " and she touches the place where the child still grows.

Colum McCann received Hennessy Prizes for Best First Story and as Overall Winner for 'Tresses'. He lived for some years in Japan, during which time his stories were published in **Ireland in Exile** *(New Island Books) and* **The Picador Book of Contemporary Irish Fiction**. *In 1994 he published an acclaimed debut collection,* **Fishing the Sloe-Black River**, *which received The Rooney Prize for Irish Literature and the title story of which has been filmed. Now living in New York, his first novel,* **Songdogs** *appeared in 1995.*

1991

SWING DOORS

MARIE HANNIGAN

Marie Hannigan lives in Donegal. She participated in the National Writers Workshop with John McGahern in 1989 and has won prizes in the Allingham Festival. She won this year's Listowel Writers' Week fiction award with her story 'Swing Doors'.

I'd been knocking about Gora taking stick all day, and I was fed up with the lot of them. From the lorry driver who lifted me outside Castlecove, to the geezers on the pier who looked at me as if I'd just landed from outer space.

The lorry driver cackled when I told him the crack. "Good-lookin' blonde like you aboard a boat? Not a chance darlin'." I had my feet wedged against the dashboard trying to brace myself as my friend booted the lorry into the corkscrew bends. When he deposited me at the end of the pier, Valerie said her first grateful prayer in a long, long time.

The pier wasn't much bigger than the slip at Castlecove, just long enough to take the dozen half-deckers that were tied up along one side, with a high wall breaking the force of the Atlantic on the other. There were clutches of old bucks hanging about and they nearly went hysterical when I asked about the start, shaking their heads at the absurdity of a woman asking for a berth.

I'd left Castlecove after a row with my father. There was no way I was going back to admit that he was right. I kept pestering everyone in sight until eventually one old boy mentioned a name, and Valerie was away. "Pol Francie? Who's that?" I asked.

"Young fella lives in the big house above the lake. Got his whole crew livin' with him."

"Aye," someone muttered. "There be's all kinds of rare ones comin' and goin' in that house." They were still laughing as I walked away from the pier.

I found Pol Francie leaning up against the bar of Charlie's Roadhouse, with a couple of other young fellows. The minute he turned to look at me, I took his measure. Weather-bleached hair and wide green eyes. Watch it, I thought. But he didn't laugh when I asked him for a berth. "You been out in a boat before, Valerie? Ever been sea-sick?"

"Sure. Been a bit queasy, but no big deal. My father skippers *McStrancher's Bride*."

"You're Owen McStrancher's daughter? Okay, you're on," he said.

One of the others gave him a look, but he just shrugged. "We're short-handed. She'll be as good as the young fella anyhow."

The young fellow looked hurt. He didn't have the weathered look of the others. I knew I'd be better than him.

I showed Pol my rucksack. "Will I stow my gear aboard the boat?"

"No need. You can kip in the house with us."

The house was a surprise, a massive old place, bang in the middle of a golf course. As Pol led me through, he could see I was impressed by the space of the rooms and the wide bay windows, built by the gentry, he told me. "Those old landlords had taste," he joked, dumping my rucksack onto a wide bed. "This room belonged to my grand-aunt. Take a good look at it now. We'll be fishing nights, so you won't see much of it."

We shot in the dark, dozing through the night by a paraffin heater. At dawn we hauled in, hand over hand, and my gambler's heart jumped to see the brightness of the salmon breaking surface.

That first week I watched the young fellow retching over the side, holding back my own bile till I thought I'd die. The net hauler was broken. We pulled in the slack quickly with the dip of the boat, holding fast as she rolled onto her port side. Only the kid tried to haul against the heave of the half-decker. At the end of the week, I bound up his raw, blistered hands. "Don't haul on the side of the boat, Jason. You'll kill yourself pulling against her."

"How come you know about fishing, Valerie?"

"It's in the blood," I told him.

The row with my father had brought it to a head. He needed a crewman, and I'd asked him for the berth.

"Haven't you got a job already." He clucked his tongue.

"I'd make more money fishing than I'd ever see pounding a typewriter for 'Silver Sails'. What was the point of all that navigation you taught me, if you didn't want me fishing?"

"You're a girl," he said. End of story.

No skipper in town would take me on when my father wouldn't do it. So I just took off. I told myself I was well out of the stinking place, though every fisherman worth his waders knows Castlecove is the only place to be, on this goddess-forsaken shamrock shore. Factoryless, pollution-free Gora will never be fishing port of the year.

But you can still smell the salt of the sea here.

My presence in the house has sparked off some speculation. When I'm buying groceries in the village shop, Maya, the owner, passes some remark about me living alone with all those men. "Maybe you'd need one of these," she jokes, holding up a slide bolt. I don't take it seriously at first, but later, as I'm getting into bed, I pull a heavy trunk from a corner of the room and drag it across the doorway.

Sometimes when I catch Pol looking at me, I remember the foreign girl who was fishing on a trawler in Castlecove. She had worked on the deck as well as any man, until two of the crew-men fell out over her. Whenever I catch Pol giving me the eye, I turn the other way.

The morning sun is climbing into the sky by the time we land our fish. It intrudes through the south-facing window above my bed. In the beginning everything kept me awake, the light on the high ceiling, the snores of the others, the swans below on the lake. Now I could sleep through the Big Bang.

Saturday and Sunday we are forced to lie ashore, chafing at the vigilance of the bailiffs who patrol the pier, enforcing the week-end fishing bar.

Jason is a music student. He practises his violin in the study. Mick and Jimmy squat in the sitting room playing blood-and-guts videos. Pol is heavy into some black blues singer. He stays in his room, his stereo turned high to drown the rest out.

Every night we're ashore, these different sounds fight for air-space till I think I'll go mad in the head.

We were fishing for a fortnight when Pol gave us our first sub. There would be no square-up until the end of the season. I had a couple of pints in Charlie's with the boys and came home early. Soothed by the emptiness of the house, I took a can of wine to bed and lay back, wallowing in the silence. At this stage I was tired of dragging that trunk across the floor, but for some reason, before dropping off to sleep, I hopped out of bed and barricaded myself in.

Hours later I drifted up from sleep to hear the clatter of footsteps on the stairs as the boys landed home, well tight.

Everything was quieting down when I heard a rattle at my door knob. The door was pushed inward, jamming as it met the resistance of the trunk.

The next day, when I was picking up the groceries in Maya's shop, I dropped a slide bolt into my wire basket along with the grub. Maya picked it up and examined it as she was doing up the till. "I see you're taking my advice," she smiled. I smiled back at her. That trunk was breaking my back.

There are other intrusions on my sleep. Once I woke to find a man looking over the brass bedhead. I swear, smiling down at me. I closed my eyes, waiting for the smiling mouth to come down on my neck and suck my life's blood from me. Five terrified minutes later, I opened my eyes — to nothing. My man had drifted out through the bolted door again.

One night I heard a girl crying, bawling her little heart out. Another ghost, I thought. But when I went down in the morning there was a long silk scarf lying across the back of a chair. I waited for its owner to appear for breakfast. But she never did. Pol had turfed her out some time in the middle of the night.

The others were such pathetic cooks, I ended up doing the lot. I was boiling my sheets in a pot on the range one Saturday morning when Pol tumbled a bundle of laundry at my feet. "You wouldn't shove mine in as well," he coaxed.

"I wouldn't," I said.

But I did. After all, the man did give me a chance. So now every Saturday, Jason helps me to light a huge fire and I spend the day hanging over the ancient bathtub.

Five weeks into the salmon, coming to the end of the season, Pol told me to order an extra load of grub for the boat. "We'll chance it out Saturday evening. The bailiffs are after the Fanad men this weekend. We should get away clear."

It was perfect salmon weather, a gentle breeze to ruffle the water, and a light continuous mizzle of rain. With none of the other boats out, we shot away clear in the best patch of water and settled by the stove to wait. We hardly spoke or slept all night. At sunrise my pulse jigged as we hauled in one hundred-and-eighty-three salmon.

We were making for shore when a voice came crackling over the radio. Pol put his ear to the set. "It's Charlie. The bailiffs are on the pier. There's a load of them heading out in the motorboat. We'll have to make for the estuary and drop anchor. Charlie will pick us up in the punt."

"What if the bailiffs catch up on us?"

Pol pointed to the bundle of gaffs at the bottom of the boat. "There's one for every man."

I looked at the vicious hooked instruments. Then I thought of the catch, the best we'd had in the season. I picked up a gaff and gripped it hard.

Pol navigated the boat, keen as a blade into the estuary. We'd just settled ourselves into Charlie's punt when we saw the enemy rounding the Point. We'd be long ashore by the time they reached the empty half-decker.

Charlie had brought two bottles of whiskey with him, and we sat in the house through the morning, toasting the defeat of the bailiffs. There was no urge of sleep on me. As the others drifted off to bed, I was left alone with Pol to sip the remains of the second bottle. He talked about his grand-aunt who had come back from America, loaded, and how he had come to live with her when she bought the house. The eldest in a house full of sisters, he was barely eight years old. "I felt like I was dumped." He was lost to me for a moment, caught in the past. Then he smiled. "I did alright out of it. She left me this place when she kicked the bucket."

He wanted to be straight with me, he said. Now the season was nearly over, they'd be starting the lobsters. He only needed two crewmen. "Jason's going back to college soon, but I'd like you to stay on in the house. With me."

He kept a steadying arm around me as we mounted the stairs, standing close as I stopped by my bedroom door. "Well? Will you stay?"

I hesitated for a moment, then I remembered the silk scarf. "I'll think about it," I said, and went into my bedroom, alone.

Mick and Jimmy came into the kitchen as I was cooking the Sunday joint that evening.

"We weren't going to say anything...but after last night..." Mick halted over the words.

"He's not going to give you the full share," Jimmy blurted. "Yourself and Jason are getting a half."

Mick turned away from the glare in my eyes. "We know the young fella took a while to learn. But you worked as well as any of us. And you looked after us well in the house."

There was a council of war around the kitchen table when Pol came in. He squared himself at the scent of mutiny.

"So you're planning to snooker us," I said.

"It wouldn't be fair to the experienced crewmen to give you the full share."

Mick spoke. "The experienced crewmen don't mind."

"I mind. And I own the boat, so I make the divide."

When they left for the pub that evening, I rooted in my bag for the telephone number my brother had given me before going off on his last contract, took half a bottle of wine from the fridge and slowly punched out the long Saudi dialling code. Manus answers the phone and I tell him the whole story, talking as the minutes tick by, and the hours, clocking up a massive telephone bill for Pol. I don't put the phone down till I've finished the bottle of wine. Then I pick up my rucksack and start thumbing home.

I stood outside Gora for two hours in the pissing rain while all these sleek cars splashed by, skiting water up my jeans. As darkness fell a dilapidated van pulled in beside me, front passenger-door opened and a girl stuck her head out.

"Hop in quick before you get drownded." She's young, with a nice round face. The lad behind the wheel looks hardly old enough to be driving. "Where are you headed?"

"Anywhere, just to get out of the flippin' rain."

At this stage my teeth are imitating a pair of manic castanets. Though there's water dripping off my clothes all over her, the girl laughs, handing me an apple as if the drenching doesn't bother her at all.

"What are ye doin' out a night like that?" the boy's voice booms in the closed space of the van.

"I'm going fishing. I've a berth on a boat in Castlecove." I was always good at lying through my castanets.

The boy grins, flashing a black hole in his mouth where his own back teeth should be. "That's a rare carry-on for a girl to be at."

The young one looks at me as if I'm away in the head. The idea is too weird, or too boring compared with what she has on her mind. "We're only married this two months." She beams across at the boy behind the wheel, who bares his gappy smile at her. "We've a caravan in the car park fornainst the big disco in Donegal town."

I take a good look at her again. "You're very young to be married."

"I'm sixteen. Himself is eighteen." The look passes between them again, uninhibited pride and joy in it.

"Were you ever inside that disco?" she asks.

"The Starlight? Sure. Every Sunday night without fail, till I got a bit of sense in my head."

"They've a balcony, an' a big round ball like a mirror an' coloured lights that makes your clothes all shiny in the dark." The girl has it all off.

"You go dancing yourselves?"

"I be askin' ones comin' out what it's like. You can hear the music in the caravan at night. I be tryin' to get himself to dance with me." She giggles. The lad shakes his long hair out over the steering wheel, doing his folly of women bit, but he can't help taking another look at her. They're so indecently crazy about each other, it would make you want to cry.

They drive twenty miles out of their way to leave me in Castlecove and when they drop me off, the girl sticks her head out of the van window and waves. I picture them in a couple of years, up to their ears in crying babies.

Maybe some day they'll push their way through the swing doors of the 'Starlight', and maybe it will be as they imagine. Not the way I remember it — married men touching you up, drunks falling over you. Every Sunday night I knew what it would be like and every Sunday night I went back. I could never resist the challenge of those swing doors.

I took a long walk around the pier to cheer myself up. One of the mackerel boats had just landed. There were fork-lifts zooming backwards and forwards like demented ants. Overloaded lorries were pulling out, leaving a wake of blood and fish. I stood watching the men working. They were huge and bulky in their hooded orange suits. But there was nothing clumsy about them. Every movement was rehearsed, pared back to the ultimate efficiency.

Coming up the town a couple of fishermen called out to me. "Where you been McStrancher? Fishin' in fucken Gora? Welcome back to the land of the livin'."

I head into the 'Harbour' with them and order a round of pints. It was worth going away, I tell them, for the pleasure of coming back to this filthy, smelly town — to the energy, the blood and the life of it. I lift my pint and drink to all of us, to our diesel-scent and leathered skin, to our scarred hands and blackened fingernails, each at the mercy of variable skippers; all of us chasing the one dream.

Some day I'll skipper my own trawler, and the first time I fill her up, I'll take her into Gora and berth her up beside Pol's half-decker.

Only that vision got me out of Gora without gutting Pol Francie.

Out in the harbour, a Nigerian ship is pulling in. I can see the slim black figures running up and down the deck, putting out ropes. I could watch them forever, delaying the moment I have to face back home. The old doll will tell me that's life. My father won't bother; he knows what I'm like. I'll keep on pushing my way through swing doors, barging through, half-knowing what's on the other side. It's the unknown half that lures me in, the half that calls to the part of me that wants to make everything different.

In the same year 'Swing Doors' appeared, Marie Hannigan began to write for the popular soap 'Fair City'. Her short story 'Sambo' won this year's Listowel Writers Week fiction award.

1991

FREAK NIGHTS

CIARÁN FOLAN

*Ciarán Folan has published stories in **London Magazine,** New Irish Writing, **The Second Blackstaff Book of Short Stories** and a Constable anthology, **Signals** (1991).*

That summer my mother fell in love with a man who drove an American car. She had been a National School teacher since she was nineteen but she lost her job the previous Christmas because, she said, she didn't believe in God or the educational system any more. So in the spring she packed up, took me out of fourth class and we moved to a small house in the middle of the country that belonged to one of her distant relatives.

From the front window of this house you could see fields and trees and, through the trees, the flat edge of a lake. Sometimes you could see a tractor crossing one of the fields or hear the noises of animals being driven along the road.

At heart my mother was a social person. She liked getting dressed up and going out and meeting people and it must have seemed strange to her to have ended up in this out-of-the-way place, waiting for some kind of news from the world again.

But one evening a man turned up at the back door holding a battered oil can. He said he had an overheated car down the road and needed water for the radiator.

"Oh well," my mother said, "you might as well stay for tea now."

The man's name was Barney and he ran a garage on the outskirts of town. He had dark shoulder-length hair and a salt-and-pepper beard and he had the name of some woman (an Argentinian transvestite, my sister Sinéad later claimed) tattooed on each forearm. He didn't look the type of man my mother would have much to do with, but my father had been gone almost two years and I suppose she didn't give it a lot of thought.

❑❑❑

Towards the end of May Sinéad came home on her holidays with her records and her boarding-school ways. She was thirteen-and-a-half and somehow my mother managed to keep her in an expensive school. Maybe she felt life was easier without someone like her around. Sinéad said she thought this new place was the absolute sticks and that our mother must be finally off her rocker. She said she would have it all out with her one of these days.

Because of Sinéad my mother never brought Barney into the house any more. But Sinéad would watch from her bedroom window as they drove off together in the evening. Then she would ask me questions. Did I ever see them kissing? Had he ever been in the house late at night? She thought he looked mean and moody. She said our mother could imagine she was a gold-digger but she would soon have to change her tune. She could tell the guy was only in his twenties and our mother was just trying to make herself feel young again. Women of our mother's age were like that, she knew. But Sinéad soon lost interest in all that. She longed for exciting things to happen in her own life, I suppose.

In the old days, when she was a full-time teacher and supporting my father to all intents and purposes, my mother would spend the holidays working in the garden, dishing out jobs to keep Sinéad and myself occupied. Now she would get up around midday and lounge about in her dressing-gown until well into the afternoon. Then she would cook something quick for us and begin to get ready for the evening. She would wash her hair, put on lipstick and do up her eyes. She started wearing short skirts and hot pants with high black boots. Once, she stood in the kitchen with her hands on her hips and asked us how we thought she looked. "You look just like a tart, I think," Sinéad said. She stared at Sinéad for a few seconds and said in a quiet voice, "Don't ever use that word around here again." She went upstairs then and didn't come down for an hour. "She's probably bawling her eyes out up there," Sinéad said. "It's so embarrassing, I don't know how you can stand it."

Sinéad kept to herself if she could help it. She did enough cleaning to stop my mother nagging, whenever the humour hit her, but she spent most of the day in the front room watching tennis on BBC television.

When we were left alone she would put on a stack of records, drape herself across the couch and light long French cigarettes. I would hang around in the smoky room until I got tired listening to her complaining about life with our mother in this God-forsaken dump.

□□□

Then one day Sinéad had a friend — a tall girl with thin legs and flat fair hair called Dolores who had a summer job in Smith's grocery and bar.

At the start Dolores would stand in the kitchen doorway, watching Sinéad eating toast and marmalade. "Don't you ever worry about your complexion?" she would ask.

"What's the point in worrying," Sinéad would reply and Dolores would spend a few minutes carefully examining her finger-nails. Dolores would say, standing there, "My hair will never look as long as yours, never in a million years." Then Sinéad would pull her hair forward and shake it out and nibble a few ends and say nothing.

Most of the time Dolores would talk about things in her school — a teacher or another girl. Sinéad would look at her, drag on her cigarette and make lazy smoke rings that rose and disappeared just below the ceiling. When Dolores had finished Sinéad would smile, at no one in particular, and say, "You don't have to tell me that, you know." Or she would just start humming to herself while she turned the radio tuner searching for some pirate music station.

After a while Sinéad would get up and pour herself a glass of water. "I'm so bored," she would say. Then Dolores would look as if she was trying hard to think of something interesting to say next.

When she wasn't talking Dolores's gaze would wander around the kitchen. If she spotted something new to her she would stare at it. The first time she saw Sinéad making toast she said, "Oh, you've got a real toaster." For days afterwards, depending on her mood, Sinéad would come into the kitchen and pick up a spoon or my bowl of corn flakes or whatever and waltz around singing, "Oh, you've got a real spoon" or "Oh, you've got a real cup." "Oh, you've got a real brain." She called Dolores Mary Hick and Dopey Doles behind her back, but most of the time she seemed glad to have her around.

⊐⊐⊐

I suppose it was because she was bored that Sinéad thought up freak nights. She told Dolores to bring anything she could find. "The more disgusting the better."

Next evening Dolores arrived with a pair of shiny curtains and a bag of old clothes. They spent a few evenings cutting and sewing. In the end they had multi-coloured velvet shirts, long loose dresses and slinky silk jackets — what Sinéad called "kimonos".

Early the following evening Sinéad closed the curtains in the front room. She lit a stick of incense and put it in a glass in the middle of the floor. Then the two of them sat on cushions by the bookcase, in their bright and strange clothes, smoking and listening to loud music.

For the second or third freak night Dolores brought two bottles of Babycham. She was grinning as she took them from her shoulder bag and put them on the kitchen table. Sinéad examined the foil around the neck of each bottle.

"Did you buy these?" she said.

"Mr. Smith said I could take them."

"Oh really?" Sinéad said. "Free, gratis and for nothing, I suppose."

"Yes," Dolores said.

Sinéad began to peel away the foil.

"You can't fool us, but we won't say a single word," she said, smiling.

Later, Sinéad said, "You probably don't know this, but vodka is the coolest. No one can ever smell that off your breath."

The next evening Dolores brought a naggin of Smirnoff.

"Oh God," Sinéad said, "Oh golly God."

What did I do? Sometimes I was allowed to play the records. I would put on an old pair of my mother's sunglasses and Sinéad would make me wait while she teased and brushed my hair until it stood out in a frizzy bush. Then I would sit back to front on a chair by the record player and put on the songs they called out.

Sinéad and Dolores would get up and dance and call each other "babe" and "love child". They would shout "right on" and "cool" and "far out". Every so often one or the other would start laughing and have to sit down for a few minutes. For some songs I would flick the light off and on until one night Sinéad made me stop because, she said, she didn't want a dead body on her hands.

During those weeks my mother never came home until after midnight, but Sinéad always made sure we had everything cleared up well before then. Dolores said we were lucky. If it was her house her father would beat her black and blue. "Parents aren't a problem if you know how to handle them," Sinéad told her.

Late at night, as I lay in bed listening to the American car idling on the roadside, hearing the low voices, and waiting for the lights to sweep across the ceiling, I wondered if our lives had changed forever.

❑❑❑

One evening Dolores gave everyone a fright. She was out dancing on her own, waving her arms and shaking her body in an unusual way. Next thing she was sitting on the floor, holding her head and moaning. Sinéad got down on her knees beside her. "Turn off that fucking music," she shouted.

Dolores's face was pale and wet and her eyes were shut. I started to laugh for some reason.

"Shut up," Sinéad screamed.

She shook Dolores and slapped her face. Dolores put a hand to her cheek and turned her head to one side. Sinéad crouched closer.

"It's nothing, isn't it, Dolores? Tell me it's really nothing at all," she whispered.

She slapped Dolores's face again.

"Say something, you bitch."

After a few seconds Dolores said, "No, it's nothing."

Her face was white. Her eyes were open, but they were staring out beyond us.

❑❑❑

Midsummer's Day. Sunlight lay creased across the floor and walls of the front room. Someone was walking around the house, looking in the windows and knocking on the doors. We sat beneath the window, listening. Sinéad held the bottle tightly in her arms.

"It's a man," she said.

"I bet it's the parish priest," Dolores said. "He wants to speak to your mother."

Sinéad started to giggle.

◻◻◻

Sinéad lit a cigarette. She was wearing a pair of glasses with blue plastic frames and deep orange lenses. She was looking at Dolores and myself, laughing.

"Everybody has to try this," she said and she reached across and stuck a pair on me.

The room turned red and filled with shadows. We were all grinning. Then we sat there, watching each other.

"This is great," Sinéad said. "We could be in San Francisco, in a park somewhere."

She was right. At that moment we looked like people in another place.

◻◻◻

One hot night Sinéad decided to move everything out to the back garden. She put the record player on the window ledge, turned the volume up all the way and wandered around beating down the nettles and the ox-eye daisies with a floor brush. Dolores stood by the back door biting her nails. She said, "What if somebody hears the music?" but Sinéad gave her one of her looks.

I was making toast when I saw that someone had left the vodka on the kitchen table. I poured half of it into a Coke bottle and brought it up to the box-room.

I swallowed a mouthful. My eyes filled with water. I sat on the floor and took another drink. Then I lay back and waited for whatever was supposed to happen. I examined the cracks in the ceiling to see if they would change. I heard the thump of the music from the garden. Sinéad called my name from somewhere. "The little bastard," I heard her say.

I thought I should test my memory. I tried to remember my father, his features and expressions, but they kept on fading and I ended up listing out the things he had left behind. "Useless things", my mother called them. And, I suppose, they would seem so to most people. For example: a guitar with a warped neck, a set of books called *The History of Mathematics*, a bag of wooden golf clubs, a shotgun, its barrel blocked with aircraft modelling cement. When we moved from the city all this stuff was dumped, but I took the shotgun with me and hid it behind a press in my room. I had some idea of using it for hunting.

I thought of a field somewhere with a flock of white birds rising into the air and my father standing in the middle, an arm raised towards the sky, shouting something I couldn't hear because of the beating of the wings.

It was dark when I heard the car pulling up outside. The house was quiet, but the music was still on in the garden. I remember getting the gun from my room and going down the stairs.

Outside, the warm air washed across my face and along my arms. A match flared in the distance. I took a few steps and the night lit up and filled with sounds. People seemed to be moving around on the edge of the darkness. Somebody was speaking in a low steady voice. Someone was crying or laughing. I stared into the light. I opened my mouth and waited for the words to make sense.

Then I felt a hand gripping my shoulder. A man's voice said, "It's all right. The kid's just juiced to the gills, that's all."

◻◻◻

My mother never talked about what happened that night, but it was the last time she met Barney.

A few nights later he parked in front of the house and sat in the car, blowing the horn. My mother watched from the darkened landing until he got tired and drove away.

Another night he switched off the engine and sat on the bonnet. I could see the glow as each cigarette he lit hovered in the darkness. "He has no sense," I heard my mother say to herself, but it seemed to me that sense had nothing to do with it.

Dolores disappeared from our lives too, though sometimes one of us would catch sight of her as she hurried to or from the village in a pale blue housecoat.

A small fat woman, wearing black canvas shoes, called to the house one afternoon and spent a short time with my mother in the front room. Afterwards, Sinéad said this was Dolores's mother. She said Dolores's mother had said that she had had high hopes that Dolores would become a nun one day, but that we had put the kibosh on that. "What a laugh," Sinéad said.

Sinéad said our mother was too soft and she shouldn't even consider talking to that awful woman. "I wouldn't have much pity for silly little girls who steal."

◻◻◻

The July weather grew cold and unsettled. Sinéad became more sullen and talked for a while about running away from home. My mother stayed in all day, drinking tea and watching television. Sinéad said that she was in emotional trauma and that she was probably planning to change her ways so that she wouldn't bring calamity on her family again.

Perhaps our parents' world always seems less complicated than it really is. But generally people get on with things and within a year we had moved again. Sinéad started day school in a new town. My mother put an ad in the local paper and opened a playschool.

Dolores became a teacher or a bank clerk and ended up living in the city.

Barney would have stayed, though. His car, the wonder of our age, would have skidded and crashed during an icy spell a couple of winters later. After a few half-hearted attempts to make it roadworthy again he would have pushed it into the yard by the side of the garage and watched it turn to rust.

He is happy with his life, though he wonders sometimes about marrying and bringing up children. He considers selling out and going into the video-rental business or emigrating to Australia or the States. But he does none of these things.

He doesn't think very often about my mother or their glory days. Except sometimes, when he gets a bit drunk, a certain memory lights up in his mind. A hot evening towards the end of June. The last of the sunlight glints on the faraway lake. A powder-blue Pontiac is parked outside Smith's grocery and bar. A woman is standing by the open door on the passenger side, running her fingers through her long damp hair. Suddenly she leans forward to check herself in the wing mirror.

Barney remembers this though he's not sure why. It could be from some film he's seen on TV. The heat of the evening, the distant water, the woman by the car, expecting the man who might save her life to appear at any moment.

*Ciarán Folan is still living and writing in Dublin. His work recently appeared in the anthology **Prize-Winning Radio Stories** (Mercier Press).*

89

1993

THOMAS CRUMLESH 1960-1992: A RETROSPECTIVE

MIKE McCORMACK

*Mike McCormack is twenty-seven and works in Galway. He is a graduate of UCG in English and Philosophy and has had stories published in **Passages** and **The Connaught Tribune**. At the moment he is looking for a publisher for a book of short stories.*

My first contact with Thomas Crumlesh was in 1984 when he exhibited with a small artists collective in the Temple Bar area of the city. His was one of the numerous small exhibitions that hoped to draw the attention of the many international buyers who were in Dublin for the official Rosc Exhibition at the Guinness Hops Store. It was July, just a few months after Thomas had been expelled from the National College of Art and Design for persevering with work that, in the opinion of his tutors, dealt obscenely and obsessively with themes of gratuitous violence.

His exhibition, 'Notes Towards an Autobiography', had been hanging less than three days and already word had got around and quite a bit of outraged comment excited. It consisted of four box frames with black silk backgrounds on which were mounted his left lung, the thumb of his left hand, his right ear and the middle toe of his left foot. Crumlesh was present also and easily recognisable; he was standing by the invigilator's desk, his head and right hand swathed in white but not too clean bandages. He was pale, carrying himself delicately, and like most young artists, badly in need of a shave. After I had got over my initial shock I ventured a few words of congratulations, more by way of curiosity than any heartfelt belief in his work's merit. He surprised me with a lavish smile and a resolute handshake that contradicted completely his frail appearance. This was my first experience of the central paradox in his personality — the palpably gruesome nature of his work set against his unfailing good spirits and optimism. He surprised me further by telling me in conspiratorial tones that he planned to flee the country that very evening. Some of the criticism of his work had found its way into the national press and already a few people with placards had picketed the exhibition. He had even heard word that the police were pressing for warrants to arrest him under the obscenity laws. He confided that what really worried him was that he might fall foul of Ireland's notoriously lax committal laws; he quoted an impressive array of statistics on secondary committals in the Republic.

I ended this encounter by buying his lung. His enthusiasm and verve convinced me of its worth and his whole appearance told me that he was in need of money. Before I left he told me of the programme of work he had laid out for himself — a programme that would take him up to 1992, the year he hoped to retire. I offered to check his wounds, his bandages looked like they had not been changed in a few days. He declined the offer saying that he had not the time, he needed to cash the cheque and he was afraid of missing the ferry to Holyhead. We shook hands one final time before parting and I did not expect to see him ever again.

Our paths crossed again two years later. I was in London, attending a symposium on trauma and phantom pain in amputees at the Royal College of Surgeons. By chance, in a Crouch End pub, I picked up a flier advertising the upcoming festival of Irish culture and music in Finsbury Park. Near the bottom of a list of rock bands and comedians was mention of a small exhibition of avant garde work to be shown in a tiny gallery in Birchington Road. Thomas' name was mentioned second from the bottom. When I eventually found the gallery it was nothing more than two rooms knocked together on the third floor over a Chinese restaurant. Among the second-rate paintings and sculptures Thomas' work was not difficult to recognise. It stood in the middle of the floor mounted on a black metal stand, a single human arm stripped of skin and musculature leaning at an obtuse angle to the floor. The bleached bones of the hand were closed in a half-fist and the whole thing looked like the jib of some futuristic robot. As I approached it the arm jerked into life, the fingers contracting completely and the thumb bone standing vertical. It had the eerie posture of a ghost arm hitching a lift from some passing phantom car. It was untitled but had a price of two thousand pounds.

Thomas then entered the room and recognised me instantly. I attempted to shake hands — an embarrassing blunder since I had to withdraw my right hand when I saw the stump near his shoulder. As before, he was in good spirits and entered quickly into a detailed explanation of what he called his "technique". He had bleached the bone in an acid formula of his own devising to give it its luminous whiteness and then wired it to electrical switches concealed beneath the carpet which would be unwittingly activated by the viewer whenever he got within a certain radius — he admitted borrowing this subterfuge from some of the work of Jean Tinguley. He then circled the arm and put it through its motions, four in all. Firstly, a snake striking pose that turned the palm downward from the elbow and extended the fingers fearsomely, the hitching gesture, a foppish disowning gesture that swivelled the forearm at the elbow and threw the hand forward, palm upwards, and lastly and most hilariously an 'up yours' middle-finger gesture that faced the viewer head on. He grinned like a child when I expressed my genuine wonder. I had no doubt but that I was looking at a masterpiece. I little knew at the time how this piece would enter into the popular imagery of the late twentieth-century, featuring on a rock album cover and on several posters. I only regretted at the time that I had not enough money to buy it.

But Thomas was not without worries. He confided that he had found it extremely difficult to find a surgeon who would carry out the amputation; he had to be careful to whom he even voiced the idea — the terror of committal again. It had taken him three months to track down an ex-army medic, discharged from the parachute regiment after the Falklands war, to where he ran a covert abortion clinic in Holloway. In a fugue of anaesthesia and marijuana, Thomas had undergone his operation, a traumatic affair that had left him so unnerved he doubted he would be able to undergo a similar experience again. This fright had put his life's work in jeopardy, he pointed out. He was looking me straight in the face as he said this; I sensed that he was putting me on the spot. He came out straight with his request then. What I need is a skilled surgeon I can rely on, not some strung-out psycho. He will of course be paid, he added coyly. I told him that I needed time to think on it, it was a most unusual request. He nodded in agreement, he understood exactly the difficulties of his request and he would not blame me if I refused him outright. We shook hands before we parted and I promised to contact him the following day after I had given his request some thought.

In fact I had little to think about. I had very quickly resolved my fundamental dilemma, the healing ethic of my craft set against the demand of Thomas' talent. One parting glance at the arm convinced me that I had encountered a fiercely committed genius who it seemed to me had already made a crucial contribution to the art of the late twentieth-century. It was obvious to me that I had an obligation to put my skills at his disposal; the century could not be denied his singular genius on grounds of personal scruples. My problem was how exactly I was to make my skills available. That evening I gave the problem much thought and I returned to the exhibition the following day with my plans.

I found Thomas in high spirits. The lead singer with a famous heavy metal band had just bought his arm and Thomas was celebrating with champagne, drinking it from a mug, trying to get the feel of his new-found wealth, as he laconically put it. He poured me a similar mug when I declared my intention to help him. I explained my plan quickly. Before every operation he should forward to me exact details of what he needed done, giving me two weeks to put in place the necessary logistics and paperwork at the clinic where I worked. I believed I would be able to perform two operations a year without arousing suspicion. He thanked me profusely, telling me he could rest easy now that his future was secure. In a magniloquent moment that was not without truth he assured me that I had made a friend for life.

He contacted me for the first time in November of that year telling me that he planned to exhibit a piece during the summer Bienniale in Paris. He needed to have six ribs removed before February, when would be the most convenient time for me. I wrote in reply that I had planned the operation for Christmas Eve and that he could stay with me over the festive period into the new year while he recovered. The operation itself, an elaborate thoracotomy, carried out in the witching hour of Christmas Eve, was a complete success and when I presented him with the bundle of curved washed bones he was thrilled; it was good to be back at work, he said. It was during these days of convalescence that our professional relationship moved onto a more intimate footing. Mostly they were days of silence, days spent reading or listening to music in the conservatory that looked out over Howth to the sea beyond. Sometimes a whole day would go by without any word passing between us. Neither of us thought this odd. The looming, inexorable conclusion of his art ridiculed any attempts at a deeper enquiry into each other's past. He gave me his trust and I gave him his bones and internal organs. That was more than enough for both of us.

On the third of January he returned to London, he wanted to get to work as quickly as possible. Five months later he sent me a photograph from some gallery in Paris, a close-up of a piece called 'The Bonemobile', an abstract lantern shaped structure suspended by wire. His letter informed me that although the piece had excited the inevitable outrage among the more hidebound critics, it had also generated some appreciative but furtive comment. Nevertheless, he doubted that any buyer would rise to the fifty thousand francs price tag he had placed on it. He understood the fear of a buyer ruining his reputation by buying into what someone was already calling high-class voyeurism. Still, he was not without hope.

That was the first of twelve operations I performed on Thomas between 1986 and 1992. In all I removed twenty-three bones and four internal organs, eighteen inches of his digestive tract, seven teeth, four toes, his left eye and his right leg. He exhibited work on the fringe of most major European art festivals, narrowly escaping arrest in several countries and jumping bail in four. In his lifetime he sold eight pieces totalling fifty thousand pounds, by no means riches, but enough to fund his spartan existence.

Inevitably, by 1989 his work was taking a toll on his body. After the removal of a section of digestive tract in 1988, a slumped look came over his body; since the removal of his right leg in 1987 he was spending most of his time in a wheelchair. Despite this his spirits never sank, nor did his courage fail him; he was undoubtedly sustained by the tentative compliments that were being spoken of his work. For the first time also he was being sought out for interviews. He declined them all, pointing out simply that the spoken word was not his medium.

His deterioration could not go on indefinitely. In March 1992 he wrote telling me of his resolve to exhibit his final piece at the Kassel Documenta. He travelled to Dublin the following month and spent a week at my house where he outlined the procedure I was to follow after the operation. On the night of the tenth, after shaking hands with appropriate solemnity for the last time, I administered to him a massive morphine injection, a euthanasia injection. He died painlessly within four minutes.

Then, following his instructions, I removed his remaining left arm and head, messy work. I then boiled the flesh from the arm and skull in a huge bath and using a solution of bleach and furniture polish brought the bone to a luminous whiteness. I then fixed the skull in the hand and set the whole thing on a wall mount. 'Alas, Poor Thomas', he had told me to call it. I sent it to Kassel at the end of the month, Thomas already having informed the gallery as to the kind of work they could expect. In critical terms it was his most successful piece; when Kiefer singled him out as the genius specific to the jaded tenor of this brutal and fantastic century his reputation was cemented. This last piece sold for twenty-five thousand D'marks.

When, as executor of the Thomas Crumlesh Estate, I was approached with the idea of this retrospective, I welcomed it on two accounts. Firstly, it is past time that a major exhibition of his work be held in his native country, a country that does not own a single piece of work from her only artist to have made a contribution to the popular imagery of the late twentieth-century; a prophet in his own land indeed. Secondly, I welcomed the opportunity to assemble together for the first time his entire *oeuvre*. My belief is that the cumulative effect of its technical brilliance, its humour and undeniable beauty, will dispel the comfortable notion that Thomas was nothing more than a mental deviant with a classy suicide plan. The rigour and terminal logic of his art leaves no room for such platitudes.

Several people have speculated that I was going to use this introduction to the catalogue to justify my activities, or worse, as an opportunity to bewail the consequences. Some have gone so far as to hope that I would repent. I propose to do none of these. Yet, a debt of gratitude is still outstanding. It falls to very few of us to be able to put our skills at the disposal of a genius, most of us are doomed to ply our trades within the horizons of the blind, the realm of drones. But I was one of the lucky few, one of the rescued. Sheer chance allowed me to have a hand in the works of art that proceeded from the body of my friend, works of art that in the last years of this century draw down the curtain on a tradition. His work is before us now and we should see it as an end. All that remains for me to say is, Thomas, dear friend, it was my privilege.

Dr Frank Caulfield,
Arbour Hill Jail,
Dublin.

*Mike McCormack's story 'Thomas Crumlesh 1960- 1992: A Retrospective' later appeared in **An Anthology of Irish Comic Writing** (Michael Joseph), edited by Ferdia MacAnna. His work has also appeared in **Best Short Stories 1995** (Heinemann), and his first collection, **Getting It in the Head**, will be published by Jonathan Cape in 1996.*

1993

TWENTY ACRES IN LEITRIM

AGNES DAVEY

Agnes Davey is a sculptor, living in Monkstown. She started writing last December. This is her first published work.

A lot of houses in that part of Leitrim were empty ruins, old rotten dressers sagging against walls, iron bedsteads rusting, window frames bare of glass. The path that once led to the front door of this cottage was completely overgrown, briary roses clambering over the weeds, only the worn flagstone at the entrance looking like it might have when the house was lived in. At the back, outhouses had collapsed in on themselves, corrugated iron from the roofs fallen between the walls, eaten away with rust.

Animals had been in, maybe tramps as well, although it would have been a desperate tramp who'd have slept the night in such miserable, damp surroundings. It was hard to picture people once living here, laughing, sitting by a fire and being warm, playing cards, shouting at children to go to bed and stop the noise.

I climbed over the rubbish on the floor, poking with my boot at broken cups. The floor seemed to be made of mud. The rickety stairs didn't seem too dangerous, but I kept my weight close to the wall as I climbed.

Upstairs wasn't as bad as the ground floor. At least it was brighter, without overgrown bushes pushing in through the windows. There was a bedstead still standing in the corner, and the remains of a wash-stand. Bird droppings on the floor, and the windows were gone, but it felt airy, basic, no worse than standing in a barn or an outhouse. There wasn't the awful gloom that pervaded everything downstairs.

I'd asked at the house down the road about who owned it. It had gone to cousins when the old man died, I was told, because he hadn't left a will. But they were all fighting over it, couldn't agree on selling, so it had deteriorated very quickly. It hadn't been empty for as long as the state of it would make you think.

Had he slept up here, in the bright room, or downstairs where he wouldn't have had the bother of mounting the stairs? I pictured an old man climbing into a bed like a rat's nest every night. Out in the few fields all day tending the beasts and growing the cabbage and potatoes. The house would be cold when he got in at nightfall, he might even go straight to the pub rather than spend the evenings at home. Then he'd probably take off just his shirt and trousers, sleep in everything else, and rise in the morning to the same clothes, tea and shop bread for his breakfast.

How many years had he lived here alone? Twenty? Thirty? Years must seem very long when they're spent in purposeless scratching at the soil, making enough to survive hand to mouth, neither chick nor child to do it for.

In the wash-stand was an old soap dish, buttons, curtain rings, and a missal. The pages were hard to prise apart, glued together with damp. Alice Hanrahan, November 1911, in brownish copperplate inside the front cover. Heading towards the Rising not knowing that everything would change over the next few years, the big house burned so that even now, seventy-five years later, it poisoned the atmosphere of the area. But Alice Hanrahan in 1911 would have known none of that; she'd have thought the old order was set in concrete, unchangeable.

She'd probably been pretty and gay, dancing at hooleys, throwing eyes at the brawny lads knocking sparks out of the concrete floor with their hobnail boots, looking to see who was watching her whirling when she did the 'Walls of Limerick'. Then when she married in here did she run a neat, clean house, hens chased out with flapping flour bags if they dared to cross her immaculate threshold?

She couldn't have foreseen the sad end to it all, a stranger standing here in the ruins of her life, picking over her final possessions, contemplating the miserable lonely end of her son. We have no control of the future, I thought gloomily, the fates do with us what they will.

In the back of the missal was a bundle of letters, worn along the folds so that when I opened them out they looked like the paper doilies that children make by tearing along creases. They were all dated in one year in the '30s, and I turned them to the light to read the first one, a pleasant thank-you from a girl in Tullamore for all Mrs Quinlan's kindness to her over the summer holidays. Glancing out the window, this didn't look now like a place you'd want to spend your summer holidays, but it must have been very different in the summer, with the sun shining on the water. "Leitrim's blessed with water," Leitrim people always tell you.

The next letter was to Boysie, who must have been the old man. It was much more intimate, happy, missing him and the fun they'd had, waiting for his letter, and she'd made the arrangements for him to come to Tullamore for Christmas.

There was another letter dated a fortnight later, surprised that she hadn't heard from Boysie. "Do you not like me any more?" she asked. "Did I do something to offend you?" But she was only joking, teasing him because she knew he just hadn't got round to it, confident in the happy times they'd had together at the haymaking and the day at the bog, and the kisses referred to obliquely in her mention of him walking her home.

Another letter a month later, puzzled. Had he only been codding her, had he met somebody else? Would he let her know what was the matter?

Then the last letter, straight to the point. You old rip, I was not trying to trick you and Boysie because no-one in Tullamore would touch me. Whoever told you there was TB in my family was lying. You could have asked me, and anyway I don't believe anyone said it, you made it up, you sour old bitch, and you'll have no luck for it.

Had she ever shown any of the letters to Boysie? But surely he could have written himself, found out that his letters were being taken? Maybe they'd planned it together, spent winter nights down the years congratulating themselves on his lucky escape from the conniving girl who'd have married him for what he had.

And when he climbed into his bed at night, in his undershirt and long johns, not a sound in the house but the wind outside or the water dripping off the trees, did he ever think what it would have been like to have a house full of children, a warm body next to him in the bed for comfort, sins of the flesh to confess on a Saturday?

The girl had been right. They had no luck for it.

Agnes Davey is now working on a long-term project involving sculpture and poetry, reproducing poems as relief carvings from which prints can be taken — an attempt to by-pass the difficulties of getting poetry published.

1993

STRANDS

TONY KEILY

Tony Keily was born in Kobe, Japan, in 1960 and lived in Germany and England before attending UCC. Since 1983 he has lived in Barcelona. 'Strands', his first published work, will appear in an anthology, Ireland in Exile - Irish Writers Abroad, edited by Dermot Bolger and published by New Ireland Books.

The girl had never enjoyed what's known as a childhood. Nor anything else as far as anyone could see. She walked with her face down, chewing at her slack lips. She was overworked and underfed, and her fingers were long and raw. Her father beat her on a routine basis, but without a strict programme. Under her grey clothing long brown and purple welts ran over smooth yellowish skin. These bruises were the only colourful thing about her, and normally they stayed hidden.

Her father was a big formless man. He stank of shit and had a red lumpy face whose mouth was never still. He chewed with his broken teeth on the awful fact that he wasn't happy. His shouting was terrible when he drank from unlabelled bottles of spirit distilled from potato, corn, who knows, maybe even straw or detritus. Of course he dressed in thick tweeds that were of course never changed. Eating was important for him. She could see him horsing in her mind's eye, cheeks bursting. Streams of stew juice dribbled from the twitching mouth corners. Continuous shovelling of the coarse food she prepared mechanically. Her hands peeled and chopped in pails of brown-stained water filled from the freezing gush of the iron pump in the yard. She gazes out of the window, yawns, hopes he won't find a fragment of bone in his swill.

A buttery sun sinks into wet dreary hills: completely depressing scenery that's all the more depressing because it's so typical. Surely this place can't be her home? Yes, it can. She's lived for a long time in an outhouse. The father has good reason for this. There's no mother and he knows the dangers as she grows older. This separation has never been explained to her. She was kicked out of the main house at the age of eight. As she grew up she sensed her father's needs and understood the arrangement. Which didn't mean that things didn't happen. They did. But not it. In this at least the measure served its purpose.

The girl never wondered about her mother. She dawdled or sat in a daze when not occupied with a fixed task. She did what had to be done and didn't think about her situation. Maybe position is a better word. She accepted her position in the way that she learned and repeated the preparation of meals and other basic jobs from a village woman. Her father had crashed in from time to time on the two as the woman recited her explanations. His daughter being allowed near any other person worried him. It robbed him of that strong *you* he usually flung around the house. "Are ye right," he was forced to shout, waving his arms. There was no such thing as ordinary talking in the house, ever. The girl felt her own words pull back into the quiet inside her head, where a milky calm lapped in the cup of her skull.

When the girl began to menstruate, her father got angry and frightened. He made signs to her from a distance to stay away. He wouldn't even allow her inside the yard. He had the dogs on his side, vicious unreliable mountain dogs that were famous for turning and worrying and that line of thing. The woman was sent for again. She showed the girl how to make rag pads and where to bury them when they were soiled. Her father was never to see the blood, she was told.

Fogerty was the man's name. The girl had no name, or maybe something very short. She was known as Fogerty's young one. Fogerty was an important man in the area. He owned an amount of land and ran the men on it. They also stank of shit. He was locally hated. Hate is a form of appreciation.

The occupation of the Island Republic following the alliance didn't change local life much. The new authorities didn't need to replace rural heads. They preferred to turn them. Fogerty had plenty of time for the leather-coated strangers who talked to him in bad careful sentences. Good straight men. Crucify the troublemakers. In return for their help he offered them his daughter.

His daughter stood along with him at the crucifixions. The troublemakers were bound to T-shaped frames with spirals of barbed wire. The villagers stood close around. Fogerty saw them turn now and again to stare at his daughter, the men's eyes narrowing, and he hated her for the attention she got. After the erection of the crosses he went to speak to the major.

There is now a scene in the main street of the village. The authorities have declared a celebration, with free food and drink. The villagers are worried, but greedy in these hard times. Hunks of dark bread are mounded in large wicker baskets. Three officers stand with a dark brew slopping from their polystyrene beakers. Obviously they don't drink it. They're just putting in an appearance. As they talk their eyes turn to greet Fogerty. He offers them his daughter. She's a weight on him. He has no hopes for her. They'll be able to make something out of her. Despite their leather coats, the officers aren't sophisticated men. They size her up and decide immediately that she's too young and indistinct to be of interest. They might plaster her with lipstick, and powder her, or dress her in red and black. But she would fall away too easily from behind all this, a small sagging non-person.

The major, a man with a face like a washed-out rag, turns to Fogerty to give his decision. The major prides himself on being a good judge of character. This, as always, means practically that when dealing with people he makes quick and unchangeable decisions which protect him from anything unclear. Vagueness would threaten his authority and manhood, which are, as it is, in bad shape. If he turned down the farmer's offer — obviously a form of primitive treaty between the local strongman and the authorities — he could risk giving offence. He says they will take her in tow. She stares at them out of her glue-coloured face. They put her in a cell in the barracks and seem to forget about her.

Days later the youngest of the three officers visits the girl in her quarters. He finds her filthy, well-fed, and quiet. He orders her to be washed and deloused. An eruption on her cheek is lanced and dressed. She's reclothed in brown fatigues. In the evening he drives the girl to the pierhead where a trawler is waiting. For very little money the trawlermen say they will take her across to the continent, to the Lowlands Republic. The officer doesn't do all of this because he cares about the girl.

She's an irregularity in his barracks. He's taking this opportunity, in any case, to present himself to himself as a bit of a character: original and unpredictable. Cruel but merciful. He has a glass eye and a limp and his breath smells of wet dog. Once across the water the trawlermen can do with her what they like. He's done his bit and she'll just have to take her chances.

The crossing is rough. The girl is kept near the anchor locker. She can look down into a sort of trench and see the dark links of chain coiled there. When the boat is hit by a squall she hears the chain unsettle. There's a stink of fishwater and machine oil, and from the start she's sick. She vomits for two days into a blue plastic bucket. Then she keeps down some tea and bread. The men don't much like having her on the boat. Unlike the officers, they find her exciting, although this doesn't mean that they're sophisticated. They just think they maybe could lie on top of her and she would disappear under them. She's locked away so as to avoid rivalry among the crew. The man who brings her the food can't help himself, though. It's nothing too bad. What her father, or some of the men used to go in for. With the hand, he says. The, not *your*. It smells afterwards from the bucket.

At daybreak on the fourth day they tie up in the shelter of a stone jetty that juts straight out from the line of strand. Beyond the strip of shingle lies an empty plain of light brown grass. The sea is squally, slate grey. As the girl jumps ashore her face and hands are cut by the salt-heavy wind. A crowd of locals are waiting on the jetty. They exchange bags and boxes for crates of fish. She feels these people might be dangerous. She's right. The trawler falls away out to sea. She follows the knot of traders to the strand where they show her off. A young boy throws a flat stone in her direction in a half-hearted way. His father pulls him on. The stone slithers over the sand near her, cutting a damp trail. She crouches down and watches them disappear in their trucks. When the motor rumble fades she stands up and walks along the shore on legs that feel light and unreliable after days at sea.

The girl's life has been so miserable and so hopeless that in one way it seems funny. Not for her, of course. But it's hard not to ask what can they possibly do to her next? The fact is that what happens to her next isn't bad, compared to everything up to now, even if it doesn't make everybody happy.

She stands at the edge of a salt marsh in the evening. The sky glows purple and brown. Blocky trucks hurtle past, leaving her shuddering and breathless. The stubble of the marsh grass is black against the silver of water and the grey of mud. The road is wide and raised up over the surrounding flats. There is a sort of walkway, a footpath, on the hard shoulder. When night falls she sees long shadows swaying towards her. As they come near she realises they are women, thinner and taller than any human being she's ever seen. Their faces are dead still and blue flames lick from open mouths marked out by thick paint. They walk in a haze of raw alcohol. They puff on black cigarettes, exhale, and a tongue of light shows. Although the girl doesn't know this, they are frows, huge women who sell their bodies to truckers. They're terminally addicted to the only available forms of alcohol and will drink cleaning fluids and industrial spirits. They walk the highways of the North, in the Lowlands Republic, clicking their heels along the asphalt that leads to the South, where it's warm.

Next morning a truck stops for her. She sees two figures in the large box of the driver's cabin sheltered from the clear northern light outside. She can't make them out. Teeth smile in the gloom. The face leans over to open the passenger-side door. A brown face, black hair long around the stubby cheeks. Eyes like tar bubbles on a hot day. Tattoo on a stringy forearm. He signals for her to get in.

They drive south on huge grey stretches of motorway. She finds room between them easily. They don't touch her, and even though she can't understand a word they're saying, there's no feeling of trouble about these people and the air in the cabin is light. They eat small bundles of dried meat and drink clean-tasting water from a plastic drum. The lorry is parked, high up on a rise over a stretch of carefully farmed land cut by giant electric pylons.

They drive into the night and stop in a clump of small pine trees. A warm moist wind carries the sound and smell of the sea to here. The small men climb back like monkeys into a space they use for sleeping. They hand her a blanket and an inflatable cushion. She wakes in the night to hear sounds of wriggling and popping coming from behind her.

The three walk blinking down a gradual slope of white sand. The sun is strong and she feels it hot on her scalp. The men squat down on a smooth sea-log that lies half-buried in the strand. She wanders on picking up a bit of driftwood with an end like three uneven claws. She scribbles with it in the wet sand, using the points. She doesn't know how to write. She knows the look of it, but it means nothing. She walks out over the empty beach, trailing the stick from one hand and then another, dragging out a broken line behind her. She stops and concentrates. She makes a big E and a stroke that might be the beginning of another letter.

After a while the men stand up and drop fuming butts at their feet. They look around for the girl, but she's disappeared. They trot over the strand with worried faces, squinting into the distance at rocks and dots that refuse to become her.

*Tony Keily has since returned to live in Ireland, where he has published two novels, **The Shark Joke** and **37 Minutes Per Heart-Beat**.*

1993

THE PATIO MAN

MARY COSTELLO

*Mary Costello was born in Galway in 1963 and now teaches
in Dublin. Her first story was published in New Irish Writing
in 1989 and included in the anthology **Voices One**, edited by
Augustine Martin.*

For a while that morning he thought he wouldn't get up. He knew
from the darkness of the room that it was raining outside. It was
the first rain for weeks. The ground had become very hard and
the grass was scorched. It was very cool this morning, the air had
the feel of autumn. He could picture the rain falling on the path,
soft, almost invisible. He thought if he got out of bed and looked
out the window he would recognise it as that silent foggy rain
we get in November or December.

He looked at the clock. The house was quiet. Now and then a
car passed on the wet road outside. He wished he could go back
to sleep again. He hadn't taken a Saturday off in weeks. He rolled
over on his stomach and faced the window. This rain had been
forecast, coming in over the Atlantic and crossing the country. It
would be raining at home too, he thought, the mountain would
be covered in cloud and the rain would be rolling in and beating
against your face down at the seashore. He sat up in bed and
reached for yesterday's paper on the floor. Upstairs someone rose
and walked across the room, used the bathroom and returned,
leaving the house in silence again. He turned the pages of the
newspaper, glancing at the headlines. Then he switched on the

radio and listened to the news and weather forecast. The rain was
due to clear the east by mid-afternoon. He could go to work then
— he had a garden to finish in the suburbs. He had a lot of jobs
waiting. He dozed off to sleep.

When he awoke the room was brighter. He got out and went
to the front window. The road and the front path were still wet
but the rain had stopped. He would go out for a paper, then have
his breakfast. He got dressed, went into the kitchen and put on
the kettle. Then he left the flat and walked with his head down
and his hands in his pockets. He nodded to an elderly lady he
met on the footpath. She lived a few doors up and he saw her
regularly coming and going to the shops and to the big stone
church out on the main road. Further on, two girls, both carrying
bags left a basement flat. He peeled off his rain-jacket and let his
eyes move over the houses and gardens as he walked. This was
an old suburb of large Victorian houses. He seldom saw children
on the road. He noticed their absence especially on summer
evenings when he returned from work in the newer suburbs with
the sound of playing children still in his head. As he walked he
half wished he'd gone home this weekend. Tonight would be
good in the pub — a lot of the locals were home on holidays
from England or America and, also, the parish team was playing
a quarter-final on Sunday. He turned onto the main road and
bought a paper in the newsagent's. As he left, a bus stopped
outside the door. He glanced at his watch, it was 12.20. He could
go to town, walk about, read his paper in Bewleys. Sometimes
he did that in winter, on the odd weekend he didn't go to Mayo.
He'd go to town around twelve and browse in the bookshops for
a while. He'd go straight to the gardening section and thumb
through glossy guides for new planning ideas or extra hints. He
liked the warmth and silence of the bookshops. He liked the city
best in winter — the students were back and people didn't dress
up as much — they wore raincoats and anoraks and strong
shoes.

When he got back to the flat there was a phone message pushed under his door, taken by Sheila, the girl upstairs. Tom Burke was going down home for the match, if he wanted a lift. He'd be back again on Sunday night. He looked at the phone number, then put the note in his pocket and made his breakfast.

The sun had broken through as he drove south towards the outer suburbs. The rain had already made a difference, taking the crisp redness off the grass. As he drove he had one eye on the gardens. He did this throughout the year and on the routes that were familiar he looked for the first signs of a magnolia or a clematis to bloom in late spring or a Virginia Creeper to turn copper in autumn. The gardens were too crowded — that was how his own customers wanted them too — dozens of shrubs and perennials packed into tiny patches of ground. Country people are more sparing in their planting, he thought, and they have more of an idea how much space nature needs. They're patient too.

He drove with the window down, feeling the breeze on his arm and face. The traffic flowed along effortlessly. He looked at the faces in the oncoming cars, men and women, alone or with families, heading into the city, all gazing ahead giving nothing away. He passed a park and a football pitch with a children's match in progress, fathers on the sideline anxiously following their child's movements on the field, calling instructions, pointing, moving up and down the line. At a filling station three or four cars queued for a car-wash, the drivers placidly staring out the windows or head bent, reading the newspaper. He stopped at traffic lights, then moved along automatically, not conscious of changing gears or accelerating. The sound of the traffic and the noises of the suburbs flowed over him, muted or indistinguishable. He took a turn and the sun hit him and he stirred, remembering where he was, where he was going.

He drove into an estate and wound his way to a cul-de-sac. He stopped outside Sheridans, the house he had been working in all week. Mrs Sheridan's car was in the driveway. He had never met Mr Sheridan — he was abroad on a working trip. A few children played farther up the road. He unloaded a brush and an electric drill and cable and carried them around to the back of the house. The back garden had a quiet deserted feel about it, he had thought that from the start, looking up at the tall pines beyond the back wall. With the side-door closed all the activity at the front of the house was blocked out and you were trapped between the house and the dark pines. He stood looking at the week's work. There was a curved border running along three sides planted with the shrubs and climbers. He had put a laburnum in the far corner and honeysuckle and jasmine near the door of the shed, held up with trellis. The day before he had put stepping stones down to the shed and seeded the lawn and now he would lay red paving slabs on the concrete patio outside the dining-room. He glanced at the back door and then at the upstairs windows. Most days he didn't see her. He felt her movements inside the house and heard the phone ring or the front door close when she went out.

He set to work measuring and calculating the patio area. He wheeled barrowloads of sand from the heap at the front of the house and laid it on the concrete, allowing a slight slope towards the garden. The sun was drying up the soil already. It would be a hot afternoon. He took off his sweatshirt. He remembered the note in his pocket about the lift to Mayo that evening. He would have to be out of here by four o'clock. He imagined the journey west, sitting deep in the passenger seat, the sun in his eyes, letting Tom Burke do the talking. Tom didn't drive fast. He'd put on some soft-rock radio station which would begin to deteriorate about an hour outside Dublin. Then he'd switch over to RTE and they'd listen to the 6.30 news. Tom would tell him he should think about buying a house, it was a good time to buy. He himself had bought last year, when prices had begun to slip. They'd talk for a while, then he'd slip into the soft hopeful phase of the journey. There would still be light when they got home and he'd walk to the seashore, counting the sheep and cattle on the way, then go to the pub. It would be crowded until the younger ones began to leave for Westport, the older ones drifting off before twelve. He'd glance around, not wanting to be the last to leave, not wanting to leave either. There was always something empty in the walk home, knowing the best of the weekend was over and Sunday was to be faced. He knew there was nothing there for him, especially in the winter — the whole area was bleak and depopulated. But the city, with its stuffed boxy gardens was no alternative either. He had had a dream, more than once, that he was trapped in a maze of perfectly manicured gardens, going round and round till night fell and hundreds of little burrowing animals crept out of their holes — squirrels, hedgehogs, moles, brown and furry — and began to make noises, at first a low murmuring but then it grew louder and louder and became oppressive until he woke up.

He stopped working and looked at the slabs he had laid. He walked across them, shifting his weight on each one to check their stability. The phone began to ring inside the house and after a few rings stopped. He wondered what Mrs Sheridan did indoors all day. Sometimes she went out in her car, but he had never seen anyone call. She talked on the phone a lot. He remembered the second evening he was there he needed to ask her some details and he stood at the back door, poised to knock. The door was ajar and he heard her inside speaking on the phone. He stood eavesdropping for a few moments, afraid to move. She said "Mmmm", and "OK", and "I think so", and then in a clear voice "I have the Patio Man here at last. He came yesterday...Yea, he's done that. He's good, I'd say. I was watching him work yesterday..." Later she came out to look at the work. She walked around asking him the names of the shrubs, listening closely to him. "I'm not much of a green-fingers I'm afraid," she said, and he wondered why people bothered with gardens at all.

"I can leave you the plan, and books, you know, gardening books are very good." He mentioned one and she seemed interested. She went inside for a pen and paper and when she returned she stood close to him while he gave her the title and the author. She was small, with very pale skin, from being indoors so much he guessed. Her arms were bare, she had a white sleeveless blouse on. She had a habit, a mannerism: each time she spoke to him she raised the back of her hand to shield her eyes, squinting up at him. But the sun wasn't in her eyes. Then, aware of the futility of the act she'd quickly avert her hand to push her hair back from her forehead. Her hands were a burden to her, constantly folding and unfolding themselves in conversation. Only in writing now had they been still, small fists gripping the pen. She held a hardback book under the paper while she wrote.

Then they stood there, both looking at the title.

"It's good, very readable," he said.

She nodded and underlined.

"It's got a good index."

She drew light lines around the title while he spoke. He talked about sections of the book, how it was divided into seasons, with instructions for the care of all plants in each season. He didn't hear what he was saying. He was aware of the moment, of the quietness of the garden and the fact that she was not hearing either.

After a moment's silence he turned away from her a little, gesturing over the garden with his arm. "It's a nice quiet garden. When the plants fill out it'll be nice."

"Yes."

"You could put a bench down in that far corner to sit in the sun."

"Yea, I suppose."

"You could pave the corner first — there'll be some of those red slabs left over."

"I'm not one for the outdoors very much. I don't like the sun."

"Oh."

"Well, you know, you have to go out so much in summer-time, meet people, expose yourself — not literally, but that too. No, I prefer winter, it's more private somehow. You can be yourself. It's okay, it's more acceptable to be indoors in winter, to be alone."

He looked down at the top of her head. She had short dark brown hair. He saw where her hair met the nape of her neck.

She looked up at him and when she saw that he wasn't going to reply she turned towards the shrubs.

"I hope I'll be able to do the plants justice," she said.

When she went indoors an image came to him of one of those heroines or princesses he had read about in fairy tales as a child. She might blow away. He might arrive tomorrow and she'd be different.

That night after quitting work, he called to a huge electrical store on his way home. The store was crowded because there was a computer demonstration on. He was wandering through the aisles when he came upon her standing at a computer, working on the keyboard, her eyes fixed on the screen. There was a frown fixed firmly on her forehead and she looked taller. When he had seen her before it had always been out of doors, under the shadow of the high pine trees at the back of the garden. He had thought of her as preoccupied but now she was intent. Tall and intent. He stood watching her for a few minutes, then turned and left.

He looked up at the sky. The sun was blasting down. A neighbour's cat walked along the back wall, stopped and looked at him, then continued on. He could hear the faint hum of traffic off on the main road, cars and buses slowly snaking towards the city. His eyes fell on the pines. Not a branch moved. A dog barked two or three times in a garden a few doors down. He thought of going away. He had friends in Boston, painting, decorating, gardening. Always wanting to come home. But Boston was another city, full of houses and small gardens and a short season.

He couldn't stand the thought of homecomings and then good-byes at holiday time. He looked down at the cat on the back wall, returning. He could always go west — the land was there. After a good weekend down there he'd come back excited, optimistic. He'd think about building a house, a small one, with two bedrooms, a kitchen and living-room. He had a spot picked in one of his mother's fields closest to the sea. He'd put in big windows to get the most from the sun. He liked heat. Lately he'd been thinking a lot about warm places. In the bookshops on Sundays he'd been thumbing through travel books on Italy. The pictures showed red-roofed farmhouses in wooded hillsides, wrought-iron gates leading into vineyards, old men sitting outside village cafés in Tuscany. Even the streets looked hot in those photographs. There were clinging vines and Bougainvillaea and wildflowers — so much heat and light that there was lush growth all year round. He thought of gardening in such a climate, of how anything was possible.

Beside him the back door opened and he straightened up. She stood in the doorway, a little unsteadily he thought.

"Hello."

"Hello there."

"You're almost finished, I see."

"Yea, another hour should do it, then a bit of tidying up."

"I have to go out." He could barely hear her so he took a step forward towards her.

"Right," he said.

"I have to pay you but I may not be back when you're leaving. Can you ..." Then she dropped something out of her hand, car-keys. She bent slowly to pick them up but she swayed.

"Are you okay?"

She took a step back and leaned against the sink unit. He moved to the door, leaning into the kitchen. She was very pale.

"Are you sick?"

"Yes, I need to get to ..." He pulled a chair towards her and she sat down. "Can I ring someone, a doctor?"

"I have to get to hospital." She leaned forward, doubled over and flinched. He looked around for a phone. "I'll ring an ambulance."

"No. It would take too long."

He helped her into the passenger seat of her car, then eased the car out of the driveway. She named the hospital, a large, city-centre maternity hospital. He thought of all those stories of drivers delivering babies en route to hospital. But this was different. She was hunched a little, still holding her stomach. He drove out of the estate through rows of houses onto a suburban road. He picked up speed but slowed again after a bump in the road. Then he reached the main road. He looked across at her once or twice. She straightened up a little and leaned her head back. Her face relaxed, as if she had come out of the worst.

"Traffic isn't too bad at this time," he said.

"No."

They stopped at traffic lights. Across the street a dog stood watching an old man sleeping in a doorway. The dog moved closer and began to sniff the old man's feet.

"Are you feeling better?"

"Yea, I think so. I'm sorry about this."

"That's okay. Don't worry."

Later they stopped at a pedestrian light to let a group of teenagers cross. The girls wore jeans and shirts and had long shiny hair. He seemed to notice young people, especially girls, lately. As they crossed one girl said something, smiling, and one of the boys gave her a gentle push. It was as if they knew they were being observed, were conscious of their beauty. "They're lucky, aren't they?" she said and gave him a start. He put the car in gear again and glanced at her. She smiled. Her eyes were green and her hair was very short. She was young, not much older than himself, late twenties he guessed.

"Yea, I suppose," he said, but he didn't know what she meant.

He drove on, stopping and starting at the traffic lights, a line of cars ahead of him. She sighed once, but she was in less pain than earlier. He wondered what lay ahead of her, if she was frightened. He could think of nothing to say. He thought of her hands sitting calmly on her lap.

"You're not from the city," she said then.

"No, I'm from Mayo."

"From the coast?"

"Yea." They were going over the canal bridge now. He glanced at his watch. "Do you want me to ring someone for you when we get there?"

"Yes. Peter is in Germany but I have a sister in Meath and she'll probably come in."

They were moving very slowly now, a few yards at a time.

"Will you go back there, to Mayo?" she asked.

He thought for a second, then looked at her. Her face was towards him, leaning on the headrest. It was calm and he noticed the green eyes again. "Yea, I think so. I might build a house there."

"By the sea?"

He nodded. "Looking out to sea."

"God."

She looked out in front of her as if thinking of something. Then, "Tell me about it, the place. What's it like?"

He shrugged, reluctant.

"Please," she said then.

"Well, it gets a lot of rain, like most of the west. The roads are bad, the land is poor. But...well you get used to all that because, I suppose, it's, I don't know...I only think about my own place, the villages and the towns around — Louisburgh and Murrisk and Lecanvey. The Atlantic is always there, pounding away, and the mountains too, Croagh Patrick and Mweelrea, hidden in cloud or mist most of the time. Everyone around there turns to the mountain every day you know — several times a day — just out of habit and a little fear or awe too, and of course to check the weather. You'd notice it if you were out talking to someone, especially the old people — they'd hardly know they were doing it... The place is very bright, in winter I really notice it, compared with the east. It's from the ocean I suppose. Sometimes I go halfway up Croagh Patrick for a walk and I stand and look down over the heather and the moorgrass in the bogs. Then these big rolling clouds suddenly come in across the sky from the sea and the light and the colours change immediately. Oh, and the wind — Jesus, it would lift you on a day in February... But on a clear day you can see way out, all the islands in Blacksod, and Clare Island too. My mother came from Clare Island. There's a story she tells, a true story, something that happened in the 1870s I think. It happened on Achill Island. The local people were out working — whole families — in the fields. There was a baby wrapped up asleep in the heather while the mother worked. This huge sea-eagle with a seven-foot wing-span flew in, plucked up the sleeping baby with its talons and carried it off out over the sea. All the local men of the island dropped what they were doing and rowed furiously in the direction of Clare Island. The Clare Islanders were alerted too and everyone searched and searched and stretched up into the cliffs and the baby was found, safe and well, sleeping in the robber's nest ..."

They drove through the narrow streets near the hospital. The high buildings kept the streets in shadow, then they'd launch out into dazzling sunlight.

"Do you know my worst fear?" she asked him, without looking at him.

He shook his head.

"Being alone. Not having children. Christmases alone by a fireplace. With maybe a dog." Then she gave a little laugh.

He slowed the car outside the Emergency door of the hospital.

"They'll think you're the father," she said, opening the car door. Then the anxious look she had earlier returned. She paused and looked back into the car. A porter wheeled her in and she was whisked away, a nurse asking details as they moved. He hung around the entrance area for half an hour, then asked at the desk for some news of her. He climbed the stairs to the fourth floor and a nurse there told him she was resting and her sister was on her way.

He drove out of town in her car. Several times his eyes fell on the bloodstain on the seat beside him, round, with uneven edges. He remembered her on the journey in. Then he thought of things he had not thought of before, things about women's lives, about their fears and losses. It wasn't the same for men at all. It wasn't harder or easier, he thought, it was just different.

He turned onto the road. He had the sense that he was coming back months later, that as he drove along the fronts of these houses he would come to hers and find the garden overgrown and a For Sale sign swinging outside. He slowed and took the car into the drive. Then he opened the front door and let himself in and finished the job.

Mary Costello is currently writing her first novel.

1993

DEAD FATHERS

MARTIN HEALY

*Martin Healy is thirty-five and lives in Sligo, where he was born. His stories have been published in **Force Ten**, **Flaming Arrow** and **Writers Forum** in England.*

I wanted a woman. Or maybe I didn't but when I saw her sitting on her own in the corner I wandered over. It started some way like that.

She was around the thirty mark, and plain. A slouched and weary posture. Her nervy eyes dipped as I wavered beside her, her whole frame tautened.

Whatever lines I used, they seemed to work because she quickly responded in a welcoming manner. Even pulled up a stool for me. I saw she, too, was hitting the lager, a stack of empties on the low table. My brother watched from the bar: pole-straight, observing my moves. His sober stare.

The pounding music and the crowd buzz soon faded away, leaving me and the woman adrift out on the periphery. Just me, the woman, and the cool lager. We talked a bit, or at least she talked. Her voice a drone in the swamp of my brain. Her now alert eyes checking me often, shifty searchers.

She stank of perfume. A kind of dying-roses smell. Coming in wafts. What the hell took me over to her? I remember asking myself. She didn't attract me, drunk and all as I was. I suppose she didn't attract anybody. Trapped there in that corner, watching but not being watched. Sad, looking back...

I made flattering remarks on her appearance. Stuff about her clothes and hair. I think I may even had said I liked her perfume. *Jesus Christ!*

A mate of mine gave me a wink on his way to the cigarette machine. A slow wink. Male. Approving. I could imagine how he saw the thing.

I curved an eye onto the woman's legs. Flesh-coloured stockings. Tights? That's right, they were tights. Nicely shaped legs, scissored always.

Suddenly, she was rambling on about something, and starting to sniffle. 'Father' and 'died' were two words I isolated and straight away these two words made me leave my drink down, stung me into momentary sobriety.

"What'd you say...?" I said, and she repeated it. Her bony hand reached for the lager often but as soon as the white fingers would be tight around the glass they'd loosen and pull away. Then she'd push her palm forcefully along her skirt, along her hidden thigh. It was so annoying, that.

"I understand," I said finally, when a long silence told me she must be finished. "My own father died too... Six months ago." I took a huge gulp of the lager and squeezed my hand around hers.

"Stop it!" she said. "I'm serious," she said. She broke away from me, her arms wrapping like bandages about her skinny frame.

"No-no, it's true," I insisted, hearing my voice become all hard-edged.

She looked searchingly at me, and, with some effort, I held the gaze. So striking, her eyes. Green pools. A tremendously vivid green.

I reached out my hand again. Touched her on the shoulder and then on the elbow. Gently, sympathetically. Her wound arms came loose, her clammy hand tentatively meeting mine. I squeezed it to reassure her, also spoke a few kind words. She just stared away into the crowd, a fiercely lost stare.

I studied her closer then. The bone profile. A glimpse of her bra strap: shocking black against the silky white blouse. Pendant with silver cross.

Suddenly, she jerked her head around, caught me unawares. Those eyes...

I tried to adopt the appropriate look as she started into the sniffling again. Her lips trembled as she raved on and on. She made to pull her hand free but I held it tight, wouldn't let its strange comfort escape.

"I know," I said, through clenched teeth. "It's hard."

I wished to Christ she'd stop. It was getting to me, having to listen to all this talk of love and loss. I tried to slip the mood but couldn't.

"How...how did he die?" I said finally. "Your father..." I kept my voice low, my eyes dropped. A beer mat on the wet table said: *HARP — The bite of the night.* Her trapped hand clawed instinctively as the word 'cancer' came out in a blade whisper. I muttered the word too, a chill instantly running along my spine. In that bonding moment, I wanted both to run away from her and to hold her close. My mind was pulsing, fragile as glass.

Only when she started to really sob did I look up from the beer mat and meet the eyes that were now spilling tears down her lean, marbly jaws.

"It's okay," I soothed, drawing her into my arms. "Sshh, you're okay."

Gaping over her shoulder, I saw a couple kissing in the far shadows. The lad's hand was up the girl's jumper. She seemed to tug at his curly hair.

I closed my eyes, squeezed them shut. We were swaying as one. I felt her tears hot on my jawbone. Her hair smelt of a dandruff shampoo I once used.

The vulnerability of her body, its tragic shuddering, melted something deep inside me and I began to tour my hands comfortably about her back. I stayed doing this, and whispering support, but the feel of her through the flimsy blouse sabotaged my senses. I was about to kiss the slender curve of her neck, or maybe I was just imagining doing so, when she loosed herself from my needy hold and edged away a bit.

She got the sobbing stopped and searched for a dry spot on the tissue to fix up her ruined face. I lifted my glass and sighed into it, then gulped. When I forced my head around she was again staring at me, trying bravely to smile. A lock of hair stuck to her cheek, red as a new wound.

"I'm sorry," she said. "I didn't mean to... It's the drink... Sorry..."

I once more offered her my hand. She hesitated for a long moment before accepting it, clenching it. The quiet firmness of her grip shocked me.

She slipped close to me in reaching for her glass. She stayed close. I thumbed the damp lock behind her ear as she drank the lager. I lingered my hand in her hair and nodded a smile. She smiled too: freely, without pain.

Her eyes, though, still unnerved me. So focused, as if reading secrets in my head. I tried to think of the right words to say but no words came. I even tried to imagine her stripped and open but that too was beyond me.

When she started to speak again I reached sharply for my drink.

"Here I am making a scene before a total stranger and — "

"Tony," I said. I left my glass down. "My name is Tony."

"I'm Regina," she said, the voice suddenly innocent. Childlike, almost.

We shook hands then, having to untwine our fingers to do so. She grinned sheepishly at this awkward linkage, looking oddly lovely as she did so.

Too soon, she was all serious again, the vivid green jewelling her eyes.

"Tony, I'm so sorry for...for crying like that." She broke off to sip at her lager before continuing: "*You* must think of your father a lot too?"

"I do," I said. "I do..." I made to say her name but it was gone. Blank.

A moment later my mind seemed to shift, so subtle yet urgent, and then, I *did* think of my father. It swept over me, all the blocked-out past. Beyond chronology, breaching the dam of lager, a torrent of fleeting but poignant rememberings. Many of the images lifelike, others mere essences — shadows. Catching the sods as they flew from his *slean*...sitting safe on the bar of his high Raleigh...threats of giving me the door when I reeled in drunk at seventeen...tramping cocks in the bottoms...reading him the fight reports from the papers, Ali and Joe Frazier...taken home by a cop in the dead of night after wrecking my Honda 50...his hooded gaze as I left for the boat, that unforgettable stare. In the space of one trapped second, I saw, or at least I *felt* all those cutting scenes. Fickle and twisted, undeniable. And then I saw him at the end, even smelt the flowers in his hospice room. The way he gazed at me through death-steady, fading eyes, struggling for last words but weighed down by morphine...the lifetime of love in those eyes...

"Tony, oh Tony," said the woman, sensing my burden. She crawled her hand round the curve of my back, up to the nape of my neck. I turned to her, my senses still swept by the heart's wave; I didn't, or couldn't, speak. Both of us sighed and gazed off into the alien crowd then, into the private and unshareable voids. Her fondling fingers felt good: remote but so, so good.

Fresh drinks. Change leaking from my fist onto the table, silver reeling.

My eyes and the woman's eyes meeting, locking: the final connection.

I attacked the lager, a trickle of it cooling through my shirt-front.

"You won't get more," she says then, as I make to rise. "The shutters are long down." She pushed her own untouched pint across to me. I nod heavily.

"Time to go home, folks! Come on!! Come on!!! It's way after time!!!!"

I force my head around. Stools on the low tables. Brother gone, everyone gone. Just me and the woman. And the fat barman, mopping close.

"I'll walk you home..." My voice low, a whisper. Still aware. The barman swiping our glasses, muttering, rocking his oiled head.

His straight whistle as we stood and steered a path out into the night.

I wake in the woman's warm bed but she's already gone. I settle an eye on my watch: half-ten. I'm bursting for a piss, my throat is parched. Staring over at the closed door, I listen, and wonder if she's wandering about in the kitchen. There's not a sound though, the silence is total. I let a few minutes pass, street echoes gradually becoming individualised. The common groan of traffic; elderly shoppers stopping for a natter; the juddering of a distant jack-hammer. *Where the blazes can she be?* I try to remember her name but there's nothing. I trawl back through the night, back through the lurking shadows. I see us sprawled on the settee...the vodka...the dirging country-and-western songs. I mull over later truths as I continued to stare at the closed door; the jack-hammer is getting louder.

Then it hits me like a flash that she talked of rising early for work.

My clothes are scattered by the bed and, hastily, I get into them. I cross to the rainy window and find my bearings. There's a lorry idling nearby, the thump of heavy stuff being unloaded. Everyone has an umbrella up.

Just as I turn for the door I spot the note on the bedside locker.

I feel my pulse start to quicken, also a shortness of breath.

Tony,

It's eight and I'm off. You are dead to the world and I don't have the heart to wake you. Maybe you might give me a ring later today? I work across in Gunn's (you know the accountancy place?) Fix yourself a bite to eat before you go — if your stomach is up to it! Must head. Bye, Bye, Bye,

Regina

I read the note twice, three times. The tone is so casual, so nice. I feel a severe twinge of guilt. Regina. I say the name aloud, sniff at the pinky paper. Fresh snatches of the night whisper through to me, then hit hard as belly blows. I sigh shakily and stare at the rumpled bed, stare all round the room, before replacing the note on the locker and making for the door.

The hall is shockingly unfamiliar. Straight away I see the telephone but I ignore it and go in search of a drink. I eye the settee, run my fingers along its upholstery as I continue on into the kitchen. A few tumblers of metal-tangy water, then a long leak in the bathroom, and vague thoughts of going for a cure in 'The Black Sheep' on my way home.

Yet when I return to the main room I linger, even flop on to the settee.

Something seems to be holding me, some unresolved notion or whatever. I notice the vodka glasses stark on the floor. A drop in one, the other toppled. I also notice Regina's stilettos over near the stereo. It's crazy but I suddenly feel at ease, a rare comfort shawling about me. What if she decided to come back early? What then?

And still I remain in the soft dip of the settee.

After a minute or two I rise, breathe in the room's smell and wander over to have a look at myself in the sideboard's mirror. It's then I see, there amidst the silver and glass and shrivelled daffodils, the oval photograph.

I lift it, instantly feeling a lump form in my throat. Regina is smiling girlishly, her right arm draped around the shoulders of a rangy man who I am certain is her father. Her face is so fresh and untroubled. She wears a plain but elegant sleeveless dress; also a stole and a broad-brimmed hat tilted sharply. She looks great. Her father stares out through countryman eyes, awkward before the camera yet obviously proud in that tender moment. A carnation in his lapel suggests the snap was taken at a family wedding. I can't stop looking at it. I even find my fingers brushing the cold glass.

A fresh sense of loss takes root in me, keener and more focused than in the boozed night. It quickly becomes overwhelming, heavy as a stone in my heart. There's no captured moments of me with my father; there's no draped arm. Memories, that's all. The mind images from childhood too perfect and painful to relive now; the strained years of my coming-of-age, of our slow estrangement, too bruised to forget. Death-bed tears when it was too late, all gone, when there remained only the frozen truth of missed opportunity.

I avoid my reflection in the polished mirror as I eventually tremble the photograph back to its spot and turn away. The silence is solid as a wall.

I push out to the hallway and sink onto the stool beside the phone. I feel so alone, so dreadfully adrift. I remember back to the night, grasp at its small and transient comforts. Lost minutes pass. I lift the directory and leaf through it, finally locating Gunn's. Almost without any act of will, I dial the number, hang up before the second buzz. I hold myself and stare at the bare white wall. *What am I doing? What the fuck am I doing?* I think to rise but instead find myself dialling the number again. A man answers and I ask for Regina. I'm still staring at the bare wall when she comes on the line. "Hello?" she says, her voice dim, the voice of a stranger. "Tony...is that you...?" I can't speak; I feel numbed, unconnected. I lower the receiver from my ear, it trembles like a living thing. The voice continues to echo, speaks my name over and over. I listen to it until it is no more, until the line goes dead and a new voice calls to me through the silence.

"Daddy," I hear myself whisper as I hang up, rise and mope blindly away. "Oh Christ, Daddy..."

Martin Healy received the Hennessy Awards for Best Story and as Overall Winner in 1994 for 'Dead Fathers'. He also won the Year of the Family short story award. He still lives in Sligo where he is an editor on the magazine **Force 10** *and is completing a collection of short stories.*

1 9 9 4

G R O W   A   M E R M A I D

M A R I N A   C A R R

Marina Carr lives in Dublin and is a playwright, two of whose
plays have been performed at the Peacock (where her sixth
play will be premiered in August). She is currently working
on plays for Druid and Holles Street Hospital.

The child leaned across the blue formica table and read the
advertisement, her grubby little fingers leaving snail tracks under
the words — GROW YOUR OWN MERMAID.

The child looked at the words in amazement, read it again,
slowly, more carefully this time. The same. Underneath the
caption was an ink drawing of a tiny mermaid in a fish bowl,
waving and smiling up from the page. Behind her was a
sea-horse. He too was smiling. The child, bewitched by the
mermaid's smile, smiled back and waved shyly to the tiny
beautiful fish woman. Send 25 cents, the advertisement said, and
we will send you mermaid and sea-horse seeds. You put them
into water and they grow and can even talk to you. The child
imagined waking up at night and going to the fishbowl for a little
chat with the mermaid. What would mermaids talk about, the
child wondered.

❒❒❒

The child's mother stirred beans in a pot over the cooker, her
black corseted behind moving in one controlled sway with the

spooning motion. Over by the range Grandma Blaize was fossicking for some long forgotten thing. She was pulling it out of the air above her head with her fingertips. The child looked at her and then the child's mother turned to watch as well, still stirring the beans, sideways now. Both mother and child watched as Grandma Blaize pulled some invisible treasure to earth. She saw them looking at her and gave them a quick smile, a dart of old gums and leathery tongue, before her face took up that careful concentration of fossicking and pulling again.

"Ara stop it Grandma Blaize!" the child's mother snapped.

Grandma Blaize ignored her. Tonight or tomorrow she'll have stepped into the other world. Once the fossicking started she was on the descent. The child liked her best at this point, the moment before going down. The child imagined that Grandma Blaize was pulling open a door with a magic thread, a door on somewhere else, anywhere but away from here.

"Mom look," the child said, holding up the picture of the mermaid. The mother left off stirring the beans and came over to the child.

"Oh that," she said, glancing at the magazine the child was reading.

"Grow your own mermaid," the mother read. "Did you ever..."

Her voice trailed off as she too was bewitched by the little mermaid smiling and waving from her fish bowl.

"Well I never heard the likes o' that," the mother said, sort of dismayed, but still looking at the mermaid.

"Can we Mom?" the child asked.

"Can we what?"

"Can we send away for a mermaid?"

"We'll see." Her mother sighed and returned to the burning beans.

◻◻◻

The child's mother was building a house on the lake of the palaces. From the end of the field of their own house they could look across and see the new house. It was halfway there now. The child's mother said it was a secret. The child wasn't to tell any of the Connemara clique because they'd wonder where the money came from. The money was borrowed from four banks, the child's mother whispered, and when your daddy sees this house he'll fall in love with it, especially the music room, and he'll come back, for good this time. Some nights they'd talk for hours about how they'd decorate the house. "Windows, windows everywhere," the child's mother whispered in the dark. They slept together a lot since the child's father had gone. "And your room," the child's mother whispered, "will be all in yellow, with a yellow sink and yellow curtains, yellow presses and a yellow carpet." The child didn't like yellow but said nothing. She wanted her room blue and green, like a mermaid's room. It didn't matter, she'd pull blue and green from an invisible string, the way Grandma Blaize did, and then the mermaid would arrive. Some nights the child's mother held the child so tight she couldn't breathe. The child grew sticky and hot as her mother whispered into the quilt about "that bastard!" and "all I've done for him" and "this is how he repays me". The child would try to put her hand outside the covers to get a bit of cool air on it and the child's mother would grab it and pull it back into the slick heat of the bed. "My little darling," the child's mother would croon as the child lay there soaked in sweat, with her mother's damp face on her neck. The child fought back a scream. Down the hall Grandma Blaize sang 'The Connemara Lullaby'; she was in the other world now and would speak to no-one but herself until the end of spring. The child lay there in the dark, growing a mermaid.

First the water from the lake of the palaces, then a tupperware box, then pour in the mermaid seeds and stir it all gently and the next day a mermaid would be floating on her back, smiling at the child. And the child would say, "Hello little mermaid". And the mermaid would sing a song for the child about the sea, about castles and whales and turtles and whole cities and families who lived under the sea. And the child would tell the mermaid all about school and her friend Martina, who played with her sometimes, and about the time they saw a balloon in the sky and chased it for hours. The child would tell her about Pollonio, the fairy she never saw, but knew lived down Mohia Lane. To make it more interesting for the mermaid, the child would pretend that she often met Pollonio. The child slept as the mermaid grew away out in the dark at the edge of the child's dream.

❑❑❑

Grandma Blaize lay in bed fighting with the ghost of Syracuse. Propped by pillows, pulling on an opium pipe, she snarled at the ghost of Syracuse. "Gorgin' ya'ar gut was all y'ever done, ya *stroinseach* ya!" She takes another puff to calm herself down after this exertion. The ghost of Syracuse was the husband who stepped out the door one day "to get a breath of fresh air" and never came back. That was thirty years ago. The child watched through the keyhole. He'd sent her a postcard from Syracuse, "Weather lovely, skies purple most every night, try it sometime." Grandma Blaize had it covered in plastic and punched it at regular intervals. The child rocked with laughter and banged her nose on the door knob.

❑❑❑

The child ate sweets belonging to her sick brother and the child's mother ordered the child into the black and red parlour. The child waited. After what seemed forever the child's mother appeared in the doorway with a wooden hanger.

"Now strip," the child's mother said and watched while the child took off everything. Afterwards, lying on the sofa with welts as big as carrots on her legs, the child slept and dreamt of a man with a pitchfork who lived under the sea. "How long?" the child whispered.

"Soon, soon," the man with the pitchfork answered. The child woke to find her mother standing over her. "Have you anythin' to say to me?"

"Sorry Mom." It was an ancient ritual between them.

"And you'll never do it again?"

The child wavered, looked away.

"Will you?" the mother said, a whiff of anger coming off her that would re-ignite given the least excuse.

"No," the child half-yielded but it wasn't enough to appease, the child could sense. Her mother was insurmountable in this mood and the child valued the unwelted slivers of her chubby torso. The child surrendered. "No, never again."

The child's mother gathered her up in her fat still young arms. The child counted her breaths, slowly, carefully. They matched her mother's footsteps on the stairs. A mermaid would die in this house, the child thought.

□□□

The child's father returned and magiced nuts out of their ears and made pennies hop. One evening he came in, wearing his big blue crombie and sat the child's brother on the blue formica table.

"I can make you disappear," the child's father said.

The child's brother puffed out his little chest, delighted to be the chosen one. The child watched, wishing it was her.

"The only problem is," the child's father said, "you can never come back."

The child's brother's face crumpled up as he began to cry.

134

"It's all right," the child's father said. "I won't make you disappear."

The child's brother still cried, ashamed he was crying in front of his father and his little sister.

"It's all right," the father said, "I won't do it."

The child stepped forward.

"Make me disappear," the child said.

"You can't come back."

"I don't want to," the child said.

The child's father shook. "You're too young for this trick." The child's father left the room. The child took her brother's hand.

"Come on around the back and play where Mom and Dad's not looking."

The child's brother allowed himself to be led from the house, his tears forgotten, his childish dignity returning. They played in the ash pit and drank water from the kitchen drain. It tasted of turnip and tea leaves. They weren't caught that time.

◻◻◻

The child got up on Sam Morrison's tractor one day with her brother and her mother and Grandma Blaize who was fighting with herself on top of the dresser. The child's father lifted her up on to the trailer and put her on the black sofa. The child's mother laughed. She wore a new dress and a new hair clasp for her thick dark hair. They drove down the lane and stopped outside the new house at the lake of the palaces. A swan glided by, a pike leaped, the mermaid sang.

The child's father went away again, in the middle of the night this time. The child's mother knocked the child's brother's head through the glass door. The child counted her breaths, sharp and shallow. Her brother looked at her as the child's mother held him while the doctor cleaned the wound.

"It's so hard to watch them," she whispers to the doctor. The doctor nods. Later the child's mother took them into the Oasis for knickerbocker glories. The jelly was gold and green, the colour of the mermaid's tail.

□□□

At night the child dreamt her mother was cooking her on the range and serving her up to the tinkers with homemade bread. The child woke screaming, her mother's boiling hand slobbering over her. The child preferred the nightmare.

□□□

Down in the room Grandma Blaize tears a map of Syracuse into a thousand pieces and smokes them in her opium pipe. She throws in the sea of Galilee for good measure.

□□□

The child's mother sits by the window nightly, looking out on the lake of the palaces. The music room is empty. She drinks Paddy and red and kisses her children. The child heaves at her mother's whiskey breath. "Any day now," the child's mother whispers. "Any day now."

□□□

The child's mother walked into the lake of the palaces one calm night with the moon missing. The child's father returned, for good this time. He skulks along the lake shore with his weak old whingy eyes. "He pisses tears," the child whispers to the mermaid and they both laugh in the silent house. The child's brother rarely speaks now and never to the child. They exchange glances over banana sandwiches and their father's runaway eyes. They haven't drunk from drains in years, not together anyhow.

ꓕꓕꓕ

When they dragged the lake of the palaces for her mother's body, the child sat in the reeds strumming her tiny guitar. She only knew 'My Darling Clementine'. C. G seventh. C again. Oh my darling, oh my darling, oh my darling Clementine, dwelt a miner, forty-niner, and his daughter Clementine. Like she was and like a fairy and her shoes were number nine, now she's gone and lost forever, oh my darling Clementine. The child sang, strumming her small guitar as a pulley raised her mother in the air, then they lowered her till she skimmed along the surface towards the child in the reeds. They didn't stop until her head was resting on a clump of rushes, a few feet from the child. "Oh my darling...," the child sang.

From the child's vantage point, her mother was not unlike the mermaid, bar the pike teeth-marks on her left arm. They'd tasted her and left her to the eels, the dirtiest eaters of all. But the eels hadn't touched her. Maybe they hadn't time or maybe eels too had their standards, the child thought. She strummed her guitar and looked away from her mother's cold heron stare.

"That's enough child," a man in the boat said.

The child sang louder. This was the real funeral. The coffin on tick, the procession, the sanctimonious hymns, the concelebrated Mass would all come soon enough. The Connemara clique there, grabbing on to her with their battered claws and defeated lumpy old backs. The child coughed away a titter of amusement at their mouth of the grave *mhuire strua* antics. She insisted on wearing her blue jeans instead of the black velvet gibble they'd bought her. They never forgave her for that. It wasn't real, none of it. Strumming her tiny guitar in the reeds was, with her mother skimmin' towards her stinkin' of goose scream and the bullin' moon.

☐☐☐

The child's father took the child and the child's brother into the dining room.

"In memory of your dear mother...," he said, the whinge gaining strength at the back of his craw. The child looked at him in disgust.

"In memory of your dear mother I'm going to remain celibate for six months."

The child blushed.

"What's that?" the child's brother asked.

The child knew.

"I won't sleep with anyone for six months."

The child ran from the room. Later the child found a box of magazines in her father's cupboard. All lurid fat women's gees. The child put them under her bed. The next time she looked they were gone. The child knew who had them. That night she tore one of his eyes out in a dream. The next night she sewed it back in.

☐☐☐

One by one Grandma Blaize pulls out her teeth. She lays them on her dressing table. They're soft as toffee. The child sucks one. It tastes like old knickers. The child crunches down on it with her own strong white horse's teeth. The tooth slivers like a soft mint. The child spits it in the lake of the palaces and eats a fistful of grass. It tastes of swan's wing.

☐☐☐

The child sleeps for twenty years. The mermaid who never came is long forgotten. Walking down a street one day, the child takes off her mother's wedding ring and hurls it in a dustbin.

It disappears among old chips, cigarette butts, an ice cream cone half-eaten. The child goes home and sleeps.

□□□

The child is in a swimming pool. It seems she will never reach the bottom, then she does. A fortress door creaks open, a flash of golden fin, the mermaid appears.

"At last, you've come at last," the child says.

The mermaid smiles, that smile of years ago at the blue formica table. The child braces herself for the watery descent. The mermaid's tail lights the way.

*Marina Carr received a Hennessy Award for Best First Story for 'Grow a Mermaid.' In 1994 her play **The Mai** was a huge success at the Dublin Theatre Festival and later on tour. She is currently Playwright in Association with The Abbey Theatre and her new play **Portia Coughlan** will be performed at the Peacock in early 1996.*

1994

NO GENTLE SLEEP

PAUL LENEHAN

*Paul Lenehan's first story, 'Blood Money', was published in
New Irish Writing in 1991. Since then his work has appeared
in **Krino** and **Panarge**, and he won the Sunk Island
International Short Story Competition in 1993. He won a
Galway Film Centre Screenwriting Award with an adaptation
of Bernard MacLaverty's story 'A Rat and Some
Renovations', which will be filmed later this year.*

The local Youth Club organised a week in the country; they laid
sixteen mattresses onto the floor of an abandoned schoolhouse
near a lake, and found three calm seminarians to mind the restless
boys. Alan was sixteen then, two years older than his brother.
But what came first, and years before, was brothers growing up,
rough-and-tumbling, naming diseases, robbing coins from their
mother's purse, rubbing dock leaves over the rash stinging
nettles made. The nettles grew in long grass behind the black
sheds, a split-level jungle of bushes and rough grass built for
brothers to grow wild in, and they did. They were wounded here
in childhood wars, suffered, brought their wounds home to heal
at dusk, or later. They fought then over casual grievances, but
soon forgot.

— Blood is thicker than water, their mother said.

When Alan enrolled for the Vocational School, things
changed. Jim stayed with the Christian Brothers because he was
brighter for his age, and they grew apart. Alan found new friends

and began to smoke; Jim read *Treasure Island*. Alan met girls under street lamps and pretended; Jim watched the night sky for stars he might remember. Alan went his own way with his new companions; Jim followed.

At first Alan suffered him; but Jim never understood the dirty jokes; or, when they gave him a cigarette bought loose from the corner shop, he got sick that night by the garden wall. Both boys had their legs reddened by their father, with a strap.

— Let that be a lesson to you, their mother warned.

That was when the hatred began for real. Alan slapped his brother's face hard, often, until tears came, until blood slipped warm from Jim's nose and stained his sobbing mouth. Jim might fight back, flailing his arms like a drowning boy, but never won. He hurt sometimes with a chance gouge, but his older brother enjoyed the potency of two years or more.

—Stop following me! Alan screamed.

No use; Jim trotted down the green lanes trying to keep the older, quicker boys in sight, a vision dwindling in the distance. Jim kept on, despite the echo in the trees of his brother's taunts and jeers: "Get your own fucking friends."

Jim knew no friends. Being small for his age, and poor at sports, he never enjoyed the camaraderie of sweat and spirit found on muddy football fields in mid-winter.

Instead, first being abandoned by his brother, he captured stamps on hinges made from cellophane: HELVETIA, SVERGE, NORGE, SUOMI, LAOS, TRINIDAD and TOBAGO. These were the mantras which calmed his hurt for a time. But only for a time; each evening, when he left the shaded room they shared — their two beds side by side — he found his brother no longer rambled through the tunnels they dug through bushes to the dark earth, where once they hid together. Now Alan worked as a lounge-boy and never came home some nights until after one. Jim heard his brother tell their mother that this week in the country with the Youth Club would be his last, for next year he would be seventeen. Jim had his premonition then: his brother's body tumbling into space with a scream which signified death. At first, Alan tried to persuade his mother to keep Jim at home for that one week; but his mother wanted him to look after the younger boy.

—But why can't he find his own friends?

Jim shut the door to his room before his mother spoke, afraid of her answer.

They had joined the Youth Club together two years before, where there were facilities for table-tennis, indoor football, basketball, and two half-size snooker tables scarred by cigarettes. Deep in the basement, model-makers cut balsa into strips of wood the shape of fuselage, and the narcotic smell of paraffin and glue hung always here.

Each July, the club travelled to some green and isolated corner of summer paradise, where the boys ran towards nature, and bought cider in gloomy pubs. Alan had already travelled away with the club, the previous summer, returning with a marble ashtray for his mother and stories of wonders for Jim. But this was before cigarettes happened, girls, growing-up. And before the hatred.

When the day of departure came round, the brothers shared the same train, the same carriage, the same air, but nothing else. Alan sat at one end with boys his own age, while Jim sat at the other end, beside Flipper, the asthmatic boy, who tried to talk though his breath often failed. Anyway, Jim's eyes were always on his brother, waiting for his hard face to relent. As the engine hauled them through the flat middle of the country, Jim passed by Alan's table on his way down the train. His brother played cards for pennies. Jim stood by their table until Alan told him to fuck off and pushed him away. The others laughed, Culligan most of all.

The old schoolhouse sat on the edge of a village three miles outside of Sligo. Yeats Country lay all around, Brother George

told them, as the ancient minibus guttered to a stop. The boys
saw a lake, and ruins, a farmhouse in a field of mud, and some
poor sheep on a faraway hill. Inside, they found sixteen slumped
mattresses, a shower room, a kitchen where Brother
Connaughton would cook frys and make porridge.

The first night seemed strange and new, with songs, and
Brother George on the guitar, and a ghost story from Brother
Damien about a boy with a big head. Through the windows, in
the dark, they saw bats flit towards the moon. The first night felt
happy; the next day though, Culligan started. He was the
broadest boy amongst them, with a flat nose and strong sallow
skin where dark hair always grew. His jokes were always funny,
and crude. He was the boy who showed them pictures of girls,
and knew the names for all their parts. Once, in the black pool
behind the scrapyard where they swam in summer, Culligan
turned his nakedness away from the crowd of boys resting on
the grass bank. He waded out to the pool's core, and Jim,
paddling unnoticed in the shallows a bridge away, watched in
wonder as Culligan's hand jerked up and down by his groin, the
river water lapping round his hips. The others jeered, half-afraid
of this boy like a man, but Jim dried himself and dressed,
wandered home unseen; the world stranger than before.

Culligan slapped him first on the second day in the country,
as they sat in the sun round the water barrel. When Jim, to be
brave and older, asked for a drag on a cigarette, Alan walked
away, ashamed that his brother was there. Culligan offered the
cigarette, then grabbed Jim's outstretched arm and dragged him
to the barrel. He ducked him deep, then slapped his face.

—Will I hit him again? he asked.

Alan stood by the iron gate, staring at the sky.

—Will I?

Alan spun round with red on his face.

—Yes, he roared back.

So Culligan did. They hiked the next day for miles around the lakes, and Brother George showed them Innisfree while he spoke the poem. They scoffed cake and gob-stoppers for a picnic treat. Then came Drumcliff, the poet buried in a grave that disappointed, neat and small like the graves of unknown dead around it. "Cast a cold eye on life, on death. Horseman pass by!" Brother George didn't know what this meant, so the boys jeered him for his ignorance, and for the smell his socks made at night, in the corner where he slept.

When Alan looked out from the minibus which came to take them back to the schoolhouse, he saw Jim still stare at the graves all around him. The wind blew cold there, a cold Jim could not feel as he examined the clay where the dead lay down. Again, in his mind, with the clarity of water, Jim saw his brother fall from high, and heard him scream. He did not hear the driver press twice on the horn with the flesh of his palm. Brother Damien, while the other boys jeered, left the bus and brought him gently to his seat.

That evening after tea, Culligan dragged Jim squealing to the midden in the iron shed where the boys shit because they had no proper toilet. Brother Damien cleaned it out each morning — as a penance, he said — and rearranged the plank over the steaming bucket. The rest of the boys observed through the shed's open roof. Culligan dipped Jim's arm into the shit up to his shoulder, and bent the boy's arm back until the wet shit touched his eyes and hair. Brother Damien heard him cry and ran down the twilit garden. Culligan and the rest ran away, heading towards town, and drink.

— Are you coming?

The other boys looked at Alan. He saw them all raised on a grass mound, the red at the edge of the sky behind their heads making their faces dark. He ran to join them. They walked down the gloomy gravel lanes, while Brother George boiled a kettle for warm water to clean the soiled boy.

Culligan and the rest found a pub where a back room with pool table hid behind a curtained door. Through a hatch they ordered pints, though they were under-age, and were served. Alan stayed in the background because his ruddy cheeks were a give away of youth. He drank lager that night for the first time.

About nine o'clock, local boys came in with girls. For a time there was silence and half sentences, tribes sizing each other up. Culligan broke the ice, having the ability always to speak relevant words. So they played pool against each other, while the girls flirted with boys from the city. Culligan stayed at the table most of the evening, being easily the best. Once, he took a cigarette from his packet, lit it slowly, then bent down to pot the clinching black. Alan pushed his cue just as Culligan struck the ball, and it spun into the wrong pocket. Alan, giddy with drink, sat there while Culligan called him a dirty shite, and wanted to beat him; but all the others laughed, and said no, because Culligan had missed a ball for once.

They staggered back to the schoolhouse in the dark, where Jim and the rest were sleeping, Flipper's wheezy breath snagging on its fall. Brother Connaughton gave a lecture about sobriety and sin, and told them all he felt disappointed in their human nature. Someone belched, and they all promised never to drink again. They lay on their mattresses in the dark, grinning, giggling, ready for sleep.

The next day was the tragic time. In the trees, the boys found a Holy Well, where sacred water ran into a pool scraped out of rock, and a tin mug to quench the thirst hung from a wire thread. In the well a trove of coins sparkled, thrown by tourists, ancient nuns, spoilt children, and the like. The boys rolled their trousers up and waded in; they captured shillings and pennies while Flipper wheezed and kept watch by a rock. Cider was bought in flagons, and chocolate for the youngest boys.

That night, giddy with drink, they returned to the Well and took white candles from a lead box. These they lit in their hundreds, fixed them all around until the grove shone like a grotto, or a pagan site. Culligan said they needed a sacrifice. Some of the smaller boys were frightened, so were sent back to the anxious Brothers. Alan told Jim to go, pushed him away, but Jim wanted to stay with the five older boys. Alan knew what would happen then, and it did. Culligan grabbed Jim, twisted his arm, marched him up to the centre step at the top of the rocks.

He held him at the edge of the drop down to the dark pool where Alan stood, in candlelight, looking upwards. Jim made no sound of pain, which might have made Culligan mad. So he proposed a test and the boys followed his lead. One held Jim down, the others took candles from the rocks, tilted each candle one at a time so the wax dropped onto Jim's bare back. He cried in a hollow way, as if he felt he was being tested, that this was the ritual entry to the world of older boys. Then Culligan called down. Alan took each step slowly, waiting for rain, or thunder, so they could run for shelter and forget. But when he reached the top they were waiting, their eyes shining. Culligan gave him the candle. Jim hunkered on all fours, waiting for the pain to bite. Three wax drops already hardened on his white skin like warm blisters.

— Do it. Culligan said.

Alan launched the candle into space. They watched it rise, flare, then fall down like a star, into the pool, where it died with a tame hiss. Alan pulled down his brother's shirt.

—I told you to go.

—Get him, Culligan commanded.

Alan ran through the dark trees. Behind him he heard the shouts and screams of the hunters. Twigs pinched his skin, bruised his arms. When he stopped for breath the shouts were distant, like echoes. Above his head he saw a star shine through the web of trees, but below it was dark, dark. A cat snarled behind him in the blackness, a wild sound that died within an instant. He heard bushes move to his right, so ran on, ran, past the clutching trees, ran to the edge of the wood, to a ledge of rock which jutted over a dark lake far below. A moon appeared and shone in the water. Footsteps, behind him, he turned around. Jim stood there, his clothes torn. Alan turned his back on him, sat on the edge of the drop. When he looked round again, Culligan was watching, and smelt their fear, and knew he was in charge. First, he kicked Jim in the shin, who fell down. Alan turned away, heard the slap of Culligan's hand on his brother's cheek. Then he turned around to find Culligan by his side. Culligan smiled because he knew what would happen next. He smashed his fist into Alan's stomach.

—Make a laugh of me now, he said.

Alan dropped to his knees with the pain. Kneeling on the ledge of rock, he sensed the vacuum of empty space behind him, foresaw in his own mind his body falling like a corpse to the stones below. He saw Culligan's fist swing back, swing forward towards his face. He heard his brother crying...No!

Brother George found his body surrounded by silent gulls, like mourners. They scattered at his arrival, leaving the broken body exposed to the sun and the seminarian, whose morning prayers had dried on his tongue. The boy's face had cracked from the fall, his skull split and blood dried in it. Brother George had studied death only in theoretical contexts; faced with the reality, he ran back through the poet's country with a pale face. He passed the Holy Well, where hundreds of candles still burned black on stones set in wax moulds, and interrupted breakfast at the schoolhouse with his thin cries.

—Culligan, he sobbed. He's dead by the lake.

Two days early, the boys travelled home on a mournful train. The Brothers made phone calls, led the boys in prayer, blamed themselves, searched for consolation. The authorities were gentle, told them such things happened: dark night, giddy boys, high spirits, long fall, no-one there to call for help or healing — such accidents did happen; but still they dreaded seeing the parents face-to-face. Brother George sat beside the coffin in the mail carriage all the journey home, hoarsely reciting a rosary with bitter face. The slow train reached its destination to be met by tears, sad faces, recriminations. Two days later, on a warm morning, Alan helped to carry the coffin from the church to the patient hearse. Culligan was buried in a graveyard made gentle by light and breeze.

Alan lay awake on many warm nights, but it was not the heat. It was his memory pinching, the vision of that brawny boy disappearing from the earth, hurled into the hungry night by the boy who slept in the bed beside his own. He remembered Jim turning to him with cold eyes, as if Alan might be next to fly. But Jim only beckoned to follow. They took the path down to the stones where Culligan lay. Jim took a rock and broke his head, to be sure; Alan did too. When they knew Culligan was dead, they watched him for some time, because this was the only death they had ever known. The red trail flowed from his weeping skull over flat stones to the lapping lake. Then they crept together into the calm darkness of the schoolhouse — back before the other crazy boys — and waited. Now the waiting was over; now their mother was content that the brothers kept only to themselves, and needed no others, yet even now Alan could find no gentle sleep.

Often at night he watched the still shape beside him in the dark, that solemn boy two years younger than himself. He always listened a long time, to see if his brother might only be pretending; but Jim's sleep was always easy.

*Paul Lenehan has since been runner-up in the Lancaster University Writing Prize in 1995, and is completing a first novel, **Out of Season**.*

1994

SKETCHES FOR A WEEK IN THE LIFE OF EUGENIA

for Bronacha

MICHAEL TAFT

Michael Taft was brought up in California. A former general secretary of the Divorce Action Group, he was short-listed in the New Irish Writing Literary Awards last year for his first story.

Monday

Eugenia wakes up as she does every morning. She will put on her robe, go downstairs and join her mother and little brother Bradley as she does every morning. Martha, the Spanish maid, will serve breakfast on fine porcelain plates, as she does every morning. But *this* morning Eugenia is determined things will be different. She pulls out the .38 snub-nosed Smith and Wesson she's hidden under her pillow and practises with it in front of the full-length closet mirror, aiming at herself. She checks the chamber to make sure it is fully loaded. She puts it in her robe pocket and goes downstairs.

Eugenia is tired of the way she is treated — by her family, by friends, by teachers, by just about everyone. Eugenia feels she doesn't belong. She feels the whole world is working against her and that a higher justice has been left out of the equation of life. Most of all, Eugenia doesn't like the way she is treated first thing in the morning.

For instance, Eugenia doesn't like the fact that her mother and brother get served a delicious breakfast of poached duck eggs, smoked rashers, venison sausages and toasted fennel bread with garlic butter, while all she gets is a plate of uncooked, rotting meat crawling with flies and maggots.

Mother reads the financial pages, impervious to her children, juggling meetings and deadlines and buy-outs in her head. Bradley is lost in his walkman, dressed in a designer jogging suit which the school authorities let him wear because Mother makes generous donations to the building fund. Eugenia doesn't like any of this. So this morning things become different.

Eugenia stares at the three of them — Mother, Bradley and Martha, the Spanish maid, who in turn stare back at her. It is like a movie. Eugenia puts down her napkin and waves her hand at the flies buzzing in front of her. She pulls out the gun that she has been hiding between her legs underneath the table, takes careful aim and fires three times. It is all in slow motion, like a movie. When time and motion return to normal, Eugenia looks at her morning's work — her mother dead, head collapsed on the table; Bradley slumped back in the chair, a bullet hole in the face; the Spanish maid crumpled on the ground, blood smeared on the wall.

Eugenia puts the gun down and starts eating from her mother's plate with her fingers — the rashers, the sausages, the fennel bread with garlic butter. It's not that Eugenia is bad. It's just that she has a lot of anger to work through. And besides, it's only for this morning. Tomorrow she may not shoot dead her mother, her brother and Martha, the Spanish maid. But then, with Eugenia, you can never tell. One thing is certain: if she gets used to eating a good meal every morning, things will never be the same. People will have to regard her with more respect than they've been willing to give her so far. It's Monday, so the day gets old early.

Tuesday

Eugenia sits on her own in the back of the classroom. Everyone else might be bored but Eugenia is in contact with the deeper rhythms of the world, seeing things as they really are, and not what they appear to be by popular consensus.

When break-time comes Eugenia doesn't join her friends — talk of fashion, politics and lowered expectations. Instead, she seeks out her Argentinian poet who lives every day in the toilet stalls of the school. There, during breaks between classes, lunchtime, he teaches Eugenia all the things that are worth knowing — the irresistible metre of everyday words, the illusion of surface emotions. There, behind the closed door of the cubicle, while other girls wash their face at the sinks and apply make-up in the mirror — the poet teaches Eugenia new sexual positions, one for each day, a new one for this Tuesday, so that Eugenia will understand that, as lovers, each becomes both and eventually she doesn't even bother wearing underclothes beneath her school dress.

When the lessons are over, when Eugenia lays her head in his arms, lying on the cool-tiled floor of the school toilet, the Latin American poet describes his home, a place where each situation has an infinite number of possibilities and no-one makes money and time turns in on itself like a perfect figure eight. How so different from Eugenia's world. And he makes her this promise: when she has mastered the metres of everyday discourse, how lines and spaces can be juxtaposed to make music of the spoken word; when she has fully exercised an infinite number of times all the sexual positions he has taught her in the toilet stalls; then will he take her away from here, Eugenia's world, where every situation runs in straight lines to right angles and everyone makes money and time gives way to old age and dying and philosophy.

For homework, Eugenia sits up all night in the local laundromat, drinking instant coffee from plastic cups, eavesdropping on conversations from the nearby tables, talk of boy friends, talk of girl friends, plans and strategies for the upcoming weekend.

For assignment, Eugenia holds hands with a young man in the park, feeling him wanting to feel her, pressing against him, smelling him, hoping that the couple playing with their child under the tree would leave so that she could have the park and this young man to herself.

Thus, Eugenia passes her exams. And with the money that she steals from her mother's desk drawer, Eugenia goes out and buys the most expensive Spanish grammar she can find and puts it on her night-stand where she can study it every night before she goes to sleep.

Wednesday

Survival day. Midway between the beginning and end of the week. It was on a Wednesday that Eugenia learned she was pregnant. On Wednesday she left the boy friend who had got her into this mess. On Wednesday she had her abortion. Every Wednesday she takes out a crumpled, over-exposed photograph of her father that she's carried with her ever since she could remember.

When she was young she asked about her father. They said he had to go. When she was old enough to understand death they told her he was dead. And when she understood geography, they told her he was buried somewhere in America. America is a big country. Eugenia wouldn't be able to visit every graveyard.

That's why every Wednesday Eugenia visits Madame Sosotris at the Leonard Street market and every reading the same card turns up: a young woman begging in the snow outside a well-lit cathedral at night. Every Wednesday Eugenia asks the same questions and gets the same answer: come back next week and see if the cards say something different. From mystery to mystery — seers and spiritualists, clairvoyants and telepaths — nothing leads to her father. Late-night seances, private astrological readings, shamanic quests and out-of-body experiences — all manner of divinations and paranormal investigations; Eugenia rummages through the dead world to find evidence of her father. Not successful.

But Eugenia believes in signs. Everything in the world is not an accident. Drunk and stoned and passed out she was forever losing things — her glasses, her money, her virginity, her shoes — but she never lost that over-exposed and now barely discernible photograph. Each question asked implies an answer, every searching implies a conclusion: cold comfort because not everything in the world is certain. Shadows and diversions everywhere.

That's why those who really know Eugenia will know where to find her: in a late-night coffee shop, after a half-eaten hamburger, passed out, head lying on the table, laughed at by customers and staff. They will pick her up, pay her bills and make sure she gets home safely. And they won't blame Eugenia for not finding what she's looking for. After all, it's survival day when everything, questions and searchings included, is midway between beginning and end.

Thursday

Maybe it was because Sally was crazy and Eugenia even crazier that they decided to jump into the strange man's car and drive non-stop to Portstewart because none of them had been there

153

before, drinking Jameson, smoking hash, singing with the songs on the radio at the top of their voices all night long, taking wrong turns, getting lost, doubling back until they nearly drove the car right into the northern sea.

Eugenia woke up on a concrete bench. She eventually found Sally wandering the deserted promenade, giving out that they were now lost in a boring Protestant town with no money, no way home and her periods were starting. For breakfast they shared a plate of cold chips in a cheap hotel and did a runner for lunch from a busy main-street café. Later that night they stumbled on to a party where they both got stoned and Sally got into a loud argument over zodiac signs while Eugenia deprecated any pretensions towards a common European culture though she wasn't quite sure what a common European culture was. When two men insisted that the women come back to their flat, Eugenia and Sally left, and staggered along the main street of the seaside Ulster town, shouting and singing and banging empty garbage bins. An RUC patrol stopped them and when Eugenia kicked one of them in the shins, they handcuffed her to the bumper of the patrol car while they chased Sally through the back lanes.

In the station Sally refused to give her name and address, claiming political discrimination, though Eugenia knew that Sally had no politics. When they were released they hitch-hiked back across the border, getting a lift in a sheep lorry, the driver trying to feel up Sally's leg and Sally trying to light her cigarette with an empty disposable lighter. All this time Eugenia was suffering her worst hangover ever, which the raw smell of dirty sheep wool didn't help. She thought that this was what dying must be like.

Back at home and Eugenia opens the front door very quietly, not knowing what excuse she will use for her absence. She walks into the house and hears voices — sounds, not words — coming from the dining room. She slowly opens the door and sees her mother with a strange man, making love on the polished oak table — plates knocked on the floor, wine glasses spilled.

She notices that they had been eating a vegetable casserole with aubergines and cauliflower and asparagus tips and she remembers feeling relieved that she wasn't home for dinner because she doesn't like cooked vegetables.

Truly, there are no privileged points of reference.

Friday

It's as though Eugenia has been drinking good wine all day. She feels light and it tastes good. Eugenia lies on her bed, staring out the open bedroom window, watching scattered clouds drift by. The late-afternoon sun shines on the red-bricked chimneys like a mid-west American landscape, casting shadows and warm colours everywhere. Eugenia just lies there, doing nothing, meaning nothing, without pretence or justification. She feels as though she's a circle — without beginning or end, constant, permanent and nearly connected. And it's not even night-time and friends and dancing yet.

Saturday

It's late night on the strand and everything has closed down.

And for a long time the universe has been expanding, ever since the big bang explosion, until billions of years from now it will stop and, due to the laws of gravity, start to contract until, once again, the total mass of everything is condensed into a small ball of matter, waiting for another big-bang explosion and the universe starts all over again, expanding outwards, as it is doing now.

And when the universe contracts — when stars and planets and galaxies hurtle back towards one another — time and physical laws will be reversed and all causality inverted. People will be born in the grave and die in the womb. A woman will give birth, and then she will become pregnant. There will be a killing, a murder. And afterwards, intent.

Late night on the strand, after everything has closed down, a young man is unbuttoning Eugenia's blouse and when he puts his hand under her skirt she raises her eyes to the star-filled sky — a hundred million stars in the galaxy, a hundred million galaxies everywhere in ceaseless motion. And when the young man lifts her skirt and kisses her thighs Eugenia describes the laws of the eternal universe, expanding and contracting forever, and she feels his breath on her, quicker, faster, excited as he fumbles with his trouser belt and Eugenia breathing into his face, feeling him inside her, expanding and contracting, urging him to explode inside her and Eugenia exploding inside herself and afterwards they stare into the star-filled sky. And suddenly without any logical point of reference, Eugenia wants to start putting things in order and so, she tells her young man they have made love on this same night before, that their meeting this first time on the strand has been done infinite times before and she promises him it will be done infinite times again. And though he's not sure what this means, she tells him it doesn't matter for there are enough lifetimes for everyone to come to understanding. So whether she seduces him first or seduces him afterwards, it's all just an illusion of time and physical laws for they are always falling asleep on this strand, on this night, under the star-filled sky, without remembering, not forgetting, both in each other's arms.

Sunday

'We give warning that a festival must be observed on Sunday and honoured with full intent, and that no person shall presume either to practise trade or attend any meeting; and everyone, poor and rich, shall offer supplication for their sins

*and observe zealously every appointed fast and honour
readily those saints whose feasts shall be commended by the
priests.'*

King Canute (Letter to Archbishops, 1019)

All the tombstones running in uniform rows.

In the graveyard at the far side of the abandoned street
Eugenia visits everyone in the world: her family, friends,
strangers she meets on the street, her classmates and drinking
companions, lovers on the strand, maybe even her father —
Eugenia takes off her shoes and runs barefoot through the long,
silky cemetery lawn. She rolls around on the grass, throwing red
autumn leaves into the air. She stretches out her arms and legs
under the warm sunshine. Eugenia is like a little girl again.

People get upset because Eugenia will not do what they want
her to do or tell them what they want to hear. She is deep and
withdrawn. She is loud and playful. She is cruel and pensive. She
is every day of the week. She lays out her picnic of tangerines
and cider and chilled coriander sandwiches and sits under the
shade of a very old cherry tree. She does not mean to hurt others
but she doesn't want to explain herself and she doesn't want to
perform. She falls asleep in the late afternoon heat, wakes up and
not having anything to do, goes back to sleep again.

At sunset Eugenia picks up her belongings. Soon it will be
morning and Monday and everything that the new week will be
but today Eugenia doesn't care. She places a flower on each of
the graves and then departs, climbing over the front cemetery
gate.

There is one grave, though, that Eugenia refuses to
acknowledge — her own: an unmarked, open grave, situated at
the far end of the cemetery. Weed-grown and unkept: it waits for
Eugenia, waiting to be filled with her dying, waiting for her to
trip up just the once. But for this evening, at least, it will remain
empty. For already Eugenia is heading homewards through the

clean, empty streets. Tonight there will be a solitary celebration. She will draw herself a warm bath, filled with lime-scented oils. She will sit down beside a fresh turf fire with a book of poetry and a pot of apple-mint tea. And she will go to her single bed and lie under the cool purple sheets, alone, not unhappy, still here, without encumbrances or debits, rejecting all lien, leaving the graveyard and the corpses and all that dying behind her.

Michael Taft presently works with Democratic Left. He also works part-time for Open Channel, a lobby group for community television and is co-director of a film production company.

1 9 9 5

JUST FINE

JENNY CONROY

Jenny Conroy is an Irish actress and freelance writer. She has been living in New York for the past four years.

The women sat in silence in the small blue room watching the TV in the corner. Sally Jesse Raphael. Eenie Meenie Minie Mo. Mae had heard of Sally Jesse Raphael but she'd never seen the show before. She didn't think she'd want to see it again either. Eenie Meenie Minie Mo ... who'd be next? There had been six women to start with and now there were only four. So, Eenie Meenie Minie Mo ... catch a nigger by the toe ... remember that ... remember they used to say that ... if he squeals let him go. Your turn ... imagine that Mae thought. Imagine they actually used to say that ... catch a nigger by the toe, if he squeals let him go. Mae felt tears start but she knew it was just hormones. They didn't know any better. Eenie Meenie Minie Mo. Four blue women in a row ... went to mow ... Four blue bottles hanging on the wall ... if one blue woman should accidentally fall...

A nurse appeared and read a name from a clipboard. A thin girl hesitated and then stood up. The other women stared at her for a second and then looked back at the TV. Mae wondered if the girl had given a false name too. The thin girl clutched the blue hospital gown closed behind her with one hand and with the other she picked up the brown paper bag that held her clothes. Her hand shook slightly and the nurse touched the girl's arm

gently as they left the room. Mae felt the touch on her own arm
and her eyes blurred up again but she shook her head sharply and
they cleared.

And then there were three ... three little ducks ... three little
ducks went out one day, over the hills and far away. Three fat
ducks in gowns of blue. Blue paper. Watching TV with their
bums bare. In their paper gowns of Marian blue, Virgin Mary
blue ... and no knickers. Mae laughed suddenly out loud and the
others looked at her quickly. Mae stared at her feet but her feet
were wearing blue paper slippers and that made her worse.
Everyone here was wearing blue paper slippers, even all the staff.
Mae wondered if anyone ever lost their temper here. Lost their
temper wearing blue paper slippers. She started to laugh again
and rooted in her brown paper bag to cover up. She pulled out
her watch. It was only 11 o'clock. She shook her watch to see
had it stopped but it was still ticking. She put it back in the bag
and tried to watch TV. An ugly woman was crying, her face filled
up the whole screen. Sally Jesse handed her a handkerchief. It
was Sally Jesse's own handkerchief and there were tears in Sally
Jesse's eyes.

Eenie Meenie Minie Mo catch a nigger by the toe ... and then
what? Throw him in the trash. He won't squeal. Throw him in
the trash. That's what you do, that's where they go. All the little
niggers. In the trash ... white niggers, brown niggers, yellow
niggers, no knickers, red bloody Indians. Red bloody babies in
big black bags. Whatever happened to the little gold feet? The
little SPUC badge on the convent school uniform ... not me never
sister. Where are they now, the babies and the feet. In a hole, up
the pole, in a log in the hole in the middle of the sea.

Three-hundred-and-seventy-five dollars. They asked Mae
how she was paying. Cash or charge. Mae said cash and handed
over a bundle of dollars. They were waitressing dollars, a lot of
singles and grubby, but the lady counted them smartly as if they

were fresh from the mint. Mae thought she might say "Are you sure?" or something like that, but the lady said "Would you like a receipt?" Mae said "Yes, please."

The nurse appeared again. And the angel appeared unto Mary. Mae knew it was her turn this time. Sometimes in small silly ways she could be very slightly psychic. "Lena Zavaroni?" The nurse read from her clipboard. "Yes," said Mae and stood up. Mae had wanted to be Lena Zavaroni once. When they were both ten and Lena was a child TV star on Opportunity Knocks and Mae was nothing except ten. Then when Mae was the world's fattest teenager, Lena was almost dying of anorexia. Mae hadn't thought of her for years until today. "In here," the nurse said and opened the door to another blue room. "My name isn't really Lena Zavaroni," said Mae. "That's a pity," said the nurse, "it's a pretty name."

Mae tried hard to relax. "Now you really will have to relax." The lady was getting cross. Mae supposed she was the radiographer, or was it radiologist. "I can't see a thing while you're all tensed up." What was it she couldn't see? "Once more, now relax." For the third time, and hard now the lady rubbed the cold gadget across Mae's greasy belly. Rub a dub dub, three men in a tub and how do you think they got there ... damned if I know. The lady looked at the results on her little TV screen. Nottingham Forest nil, Wolverhampton one. "OK, that's better," she said and Mae held her breath. Would she see the screen herself? Would she see a brown-skinned boy with knotty hair and a sideways smile and a coloured woollen jumper that Mae might one day knit. Then she would get up and leave and just go home. The lady switched off the screen and handed Mae her file. "That's fine," she said, "just wait outside, a nurse will be right with you."

"You know why you want this baby?" This is what Mae's friend had said. "You want it because it'll be black and gorgeous and you can dress it up in colouredy jumpers and braid its hair." That's what Mae's friend had said and she was right. That's not a good enough reason. That's no reason to have a baby. To bring a soft, damp, warm-smelling baby into the world. By yourself. Just because you can't think of anything better to do. Mae sat on a chair in the corridor. Mae looked pink and stout in the blue paper shoes. They looked pregnant. Think up a reason. What's a good enough reason?

The nurse arrived. A different one to the last one. This one had beautiful hair. A million beaded braids like pretty coloured snakes swung around her dark brown face. She took Mae's file and led her to another blue room. "I like your hair," Mae said. The nurse said "Thank you." Then she laughed. "Actually they're extensions," she said. "I've lost two already." Mae pulled at her own short hair. "I've lost all mine," she said. The nurse laughed again and lifted Mae's legs into the stirrups. "You're Irish?" she said. No, just good at accents. "Yes," said Mae, "I'm Irish." "The luck of the Irish," said the nurse and they both smiled. "My mother's from Longford," the nurse said then. "Longford, you know it?" "Yes," said Mae. "Black-Irish, that's me," said the nurse.

The doctor came in and made small jokes from between Mae's legs. Neither the time nor the place. He seemed large and inappropriate and Mae tried to ignore. But he was having trouble navigating. Why so tense he wondered ... hardly her first gynaecological exam. All amateurs till yourself Doc. "Actually it is," Mae said. She tried to relax. Longford ... imagine ... She was covered from the waist up so she tried to disown the bottom half. Not the first time. Longford. That nurse was one lucky girl, Mae thought ... that her mother left Longford. Mae laughed and the doctor nodded. Pretty silly jokes but they always worked. "General or local," he said. Both. "General," she said. May as well get her money's worth.

"Breathe deep," the nurse said. She put the mask on Mae's face. The General. "You won't feel a thing," the doctor said from above. That's what they all say. That's what they should say. "Breathe deep," said the nurse. Her strong hand squeezed Mae's shoulder briefly. "Here it comes." Here it comes. Deep breath.

Bye, bye. Bye, bye. Bye, bye Miss American Pie, bye, bye blackbird, black boy, brown girl in the ring. Tra la la la la la baby. Bye bye baby, baby good-bye ... no it's not working, better go home now. Just go home now. Go home and knit ... four and twenty blackberries ... say your prayers girl ... good girl ... The fruit of thy womb good girl ... now and at the hour and they know not what they do. I know not what they do, what I do. The Angel declared unto Mae, "She's on her way, doctor." No way, no way, no way José. She's not going. Not in the name of the Father and the sun and the holy toast. Soul on toast. Mae laughed and sat up. She reached for the nurse's hand to go to Longford but she missed and slipped instead, head first and backwards. Boom. Out.

Mae felt the pain before they woke her and she woke up crying. Cry baby cry, wipe your little eye. But she couldn't stop. She cried far too loud in a room full of other blue women lying on trolleys. Loud angry crying like a little boy abandoned. She wanted to cry out a name but she couldn't think of the right one. A nurse came, a stern, no-nonsense nurse but Mae still cried. She cried all over the blue paper gown and the blue paper sheet and even the blue paper shoes when they made her get up and go to the bathroom. She didn't want to leave. She wanted to stay with the other blue women and cry and she cried all over the red blood as it flowed into the great big pad they'd given her to mop herself up with. She cried along the avenue and into the subway station and onto the train. It was full of people and everyone stared. I made you look I made you stare I made you lose your underwear. Mae's were drenched by the time she got home. "Go home and go to bed," they'd said. "Sleep for a while, you'll be fine."

Mae went to bed and slept for a long time and when she got up she was fine. Just fine.

1995

SIGHTINGS OF BONO

GERRY BEIRNE

Gerry Beirne lives in Moville, Co Donegal. His stories have appeared in **Stet, Fiction,** *and* **Passages.** *He completed a Master of Fine Arts in Creative Writing at Eastern Washington University in 1993.*

ELLEN saw him first coming out of the toilet in Kehoes. She was sitting up at the bar sipping from her glass of Guinness looking at the crossword in the *Irish Times.* She was unable to solve a single clue. "It's a heartache," she said. "A real torment." And that was when she saw him. The first thing she noticed was that he didn't have to stoop coming up through the low doorway like everyone else. It had never occurred to her before that Bono should be small. His height had never been a consideration. He passed by the back of her stool without so much as a glance in her direction. She watched him head back through the bar and walk out in to the sunlight. The yellow glare surrounded his body like a neon tube. Like an electric God, she thought. Like a tiny electric God.

Two days later she saw him again. He was standing outside McDonalds on O'Connell Street. His hands were buried in the pockets of his dark blue coat. It looked like something from Oxfam. He looked like something from Oxfam. It's his prerogative, she thought. The Bonos of this world must have their prerogatives. Unbeknownst to herself she had spoken her thoughts aloud. Bono's head half-turned in her direction as if he had heard everything she had said or as if he had a crick in his neck. Ellen blushed. Then he pushed his way through the doors of the fast-food restaurant without taking his hands from his pockets. She stood outside and watched him take his place in the queue. She found herself being jostled by other customers entering and leaving and moved aside to allow them access. She took one last look in, but already he was swallowed up.

Ellen worked in a boutique on South Great George's Street that was forever holding closing-down sales and changing its name. "Sometimes I don't know where I work," she said. "Sometimes none of us are certain we exist at all." But all the same she liked it there. She liked the uncertainty of her existence.

The third time she saw him she was on her way home from the boutique. She had just turned the corner of Grafton Street onto Nassau Street and was heading down past the Tax Office when one of those horse-drawn carriages she had often seen parked at the Green came trotting around the corner. And there he was standing aloft in the carriage, holding a camcorder to his right eye, his body swaying as if maintaining or losing his balance. Ellen saw the camera sweep past her, and then she saw someone she presumed must be The Edge sitting opposite him pulling at the bottom of his jacket endeavouring to get him to sit back down. Tonight, Ellen thought, he will put the cassette into his video, and he will see me swooping past him in a blur. "There I am," she said unawares she was speaking aloud again, oblivious to all who turned to stare at her. And then as the carriage disappeared, "There I go."

The strange thing, she thought in bed that night, is that I don't particularly like U2. I have never really listened to their music. And even yet I would not buy an album of theirs. I would as soon buy one of Mary Black's or Sharon Shannon's. Perhaps, at a push, The Waterboys. And as for Bono, he has never meant anything to me at all. Seeing him should be no different that seeing an old classmate I never really knew. It should be a sighting of no real significance whatsoever.

For a week she didn't see him again. It was more than she could bear. Everywhere she went she found herself watching out for him. Some evenings she even went back to Kehoes for a glass of Guinness by herself, and when he failed to show up there she would walk all the way up to O'Connell Street and stand outside McDonalds, or wait outside the Tax Office on Nassau Street. It was pathetic. She was like a fourteen-year-old teenybopper. Or worse than that, a groupie.

She had become something she had no idea she was capable of being. There was a part of her that was no longer hers to control, a part that Bono seemed to have taken possession of. At night she would lie awake wondering where it all would end. At what point would she begin pestering his record company and camping outside his house in Killiney?

She decided to confide in Janice. Janice was someone who would put her straight, someone who would know how to deal with people like Bono. She arranged to meet her in Marx Bros café. It seemed an apt place to discuss the situation she found herself in. She got there early and had already finished her coffee by the time Janice arrived. "I'll get you another," Janice said. But Ellen refused. "It doesn't do my bladder any favours." She bit her bottom lip and shrugged. She would have liked another coffee. She had no idea why she had said what she did. These were not words she would normally use.

While Janice got her own coffee Ellen surveyed the room. He was nowhere to be seen. "He will turn up," she said just as Janice sat back down. "Who?" Janice asked, blowing the hot coffee in her mug. Ellen watched the steam whirl into the air like a typhoon. It spun rapidly across the room and disappeared through the open door. "Who what?" she asked. "Who will turn up? You said 'He will turn up'." Janice stared at her and waited for an answer. Ellen did not realise she had said this aloud. She was caught off-guard, and now she felt obliged to answer. "Bono," she said, and immediately felt foolish. This was not the way this conversation was intended to go.

Janice laughed. Ellen watched Janice's cheeks wrinkle up as she did. It make her skin look old, and Ellen wondered if it ever made her feel old. She wished she had a coffee now. She would have liked something to hold onto. Ellen thought she might fall off her chair any moment. "I've seen him," she said, by way of confirming the seriousness of all she had just said. "Everybody has," Janice said laughing again. Ellen felt her skin tighten. "People see him all over the place." "But three times in the one week?" Ellen asked. "I saw him three times in the one week." "Yes," Janice said. "Some even see him three times in the one week. It is not so unusual."

She took a sip of her coffee. She wondered what this was all about. "Dublin's a small town, you know. Did I ever tell you, I saw him once in a lingerie store just before Christmas?" But Ellen was no longer listening. Over Janice's left shoulder she saw him pass by the window of the café. She decided to say nothing. Janice would simply not understand.

Later that evening Ellen stopped outside Tele-Rentals and looked in through the window at the vast array of screens. She could hear nothing, but she saw them flash with the flickering strobe of MTV. A tall skinny female singer Ellen did not know danced through a dangling forest. Ellen sighed and scratched her nose. It looked for all the world like an advertisement for anorexia.

She waited patiently for the song to finish. And then, just as she had known it would happen, the colour disappeared, the screens turned to black and white, and Bono, with wings attached to his back, descended from the skies, and alighted on a large stone statue.

Ellen saw him fourteen times over the next six weeks. She recorded each sighting in her diary. She noted the time and location she saw him at, what he was wearing, and what he was doing. She had no idea what relevance these sightings had. In truth, they were rather uneventful. She felt no sense of excitement or pleasure, just relief. But what she was being relieved from she did not know. She thought it possible that she was being relieved from herself.

Watching out for him became a full-time job. She carried her diary everywhere with her. It began to affect her work. Her boss eventually took her aside during one of their coffee breaks and asked her if everything was okay. Ellen told her everything was just fine. Her boss smiled and said, "It's just that you seem distracted, that's all. It's not good to be distracted. Distraction loses sales." Ellen smiled back at her and glanced quickly out the window.

Her eating and sleeping patterns were affected also. She began to rely on convenience food more and more. At lunch she would often buy a sandwich and eat it while walking the streets looking all about her.

Sometimes she would forego it altogether. And at night she would lie awake recalling all the times she had seen him and imagining all the times she had not because she was looking in a different direction.

One lunch-time she bumped into Janice by accident. Janice looked her over from her head to her toes and screwed her forehead and eyebrows up as if considering some immense scientific problem. "My God, Ellen, you're looking terrible," she said. "What on earth's the matter?" Ellen tried to think of something funny to say to make light of it, but as soon as she opened her mouth she started to cry. Janice put her arm around her shoulder and drew Ellen to her. "Come on," she said. "We'll get a drink."

Ellen took out her diary and showed it to Janice. Then she carefully recounted each sighting from the beginning. Janice listened to every word and examined each entry. "You're sure it was him?" she asked when Ellen had finished. "Of course, I'm sure." Ellen pulled a hair from her tongue. "Do you think I'm imagining all of this? Do you think I'm making it all up?" She couldn't believe Janice could think such a thing. Janice squeezed her arm. "I'm sorry," she said. "I just thought that, maybe, it was someone else who looked like him. That's all. Such a thing is possible." "I know what he looks like," Ellen said. And then she thought, we don't know each other. I don't know Janice, and Janice does not know me. We are not the people each of us thinks we are. "Everybody knows what he looks like. I wouldn't mistake him. I'm sure of it." Ellen took a sip from her gin and tonic. She held it in her mouth like a thought, then swallowed it. "And even if it wasn't him, would that matter? Even if it was somebody else I was seeing, is it not strange? Is it not particularly odd?"

And Janice had to agree that fourteen times in six weeks was an exceptional amount of sightings. "Perhaps he's following you." Ellen thought this the most ridiculous remark she had ever heard. "Why on earth should he want to follow me? After all this is one of the most famous men in the world." Janice shrugged. "I've no idea," she said. "But it would provide some sort of explanation." Ellen shivered, and her arms erupted in goose-bumps. "Ask him," Janice said, finishing off her coffee and tapping the tip of her little finger on the table for no apparent reason. "The next time you see him, ask him."

Ellen saw his head and shoulders through one of the side windows on the top deck of the 46A. It was stopped at the lights at the corner of College Street. Just as she reached into her pocket for her diary she saw him turn around in his seat and look out through the window down at the street below. He seemed to be staring straight at her. She thought she saw him smile. Ellen fought an urge to wave. Then the lights changed, and the traffic moved off again.

Ellen woke up at two in the morning. She was drenched in sweat. She tried to sit up in bed but was unable to move. Ellen realised she could not feel the lower half of her body. It was as if it no longer existed. She pulled the sheets up and looked beneath them. Her legs were still there and looked the same as usual. She reached down with her hand and touched her left thigh. Despite the perspiration that coated her upper body and soaked into the sheets, her thigh felt cold and rubbery, like left-over spaghetti. And although she could feel her thigh with her fingers she had no sensation in it at all. This is how Elvis must have felt, she thought, on the Ed Sullivan Show when they would only film him from the waist up. And then she wondered how she knew anything about Elvis and the Ed Sullivan Show. "There are things about me," she said, "that even I don't know."

Her body jerked, and she cried out as a long series of sharp jabs shot through her toes as if someone was pushing needles into the soft fleshy pads beneath them. Then slowly the lower part of her body regained its sensation.

Her boss issued a final warning. She told her she would be sorry to see her leave, that she had high hopes for her, she had even planned to make her assistant manageress very soon, but if she didn't start showing more interest in her work, she would have to let her go. She said she had no idea what had gotten into her.

Ellen said she understood, and that she had no idea what had gotten into her either. She said she hoped that things would soon return to normal.

That night Ellen's lower body numbed and seemed to be absent once more. What if it spreads, she thought? What if I disappear altogether?

Ellen and the other assistants refolded and restacked the clothes that had been taken down and then discarded. It was five minutes to closing time. She wondered if she would go straight home that evening or stop by one of the many places she had previously sighted him in. She held a mauve cashmere jumper in her hand. She brought it to her face and rubbed it against her. The door squeaked open as a late customer arrived. One of the girls groaned. "We're closing," she called out without bothering to look up. No one looked up. None of them wanted to get involved at this late stage. Ellen sighed. It may as well be her. She breathed in, extended her lips into a smile, turned around and asked, "Can I help you?" "Yes," he answered, "I believe you can."

Ellen's mouth went dry. Her eyes glazed over and lost focus, and the tips of her earlobes burned. The excited muttering of the other assistants buzzed about her ears like insects. "I'm looking for a gift," he said smiling and looking her right in the eyes. "Something special." Ellen could only nod. She was incapable of speaking. He ran his fingers back through his dark hair. "Have you any suggestions?" He continued to look her in the eyes. Ellen felt her pupils expanding and contracting. She leaned back and steadied herself against the counter. "It's for a lady. A very special lady." "Hmmm," Ellen said, grateful for any sound she could make. Then she wet her lips and said, "I see." He pulled the sleeve of his jacket halfways up his arm. She looked at the mass of black hairs that were revealed, and she noticed he had hairs on his fingers also. Again he smiled. "I'm sure you'll know exactly what she desires." Ellen thought of his wife, Ali, petite and beautiful, and she thought of all the supermodels he surrounded himself with in the photos in the papers, and she thought of herself leaning against the counter in a small boutique on South Great George's Street, whose name she no longer could remember, with insects buzzing about her ears and her pupils expanding and contracting, and then she thought of herself sweating beneath the glare of the lights on the Ed Sullivan Show with a large microphone in one hand and the other cupped to her ear, belting out the raucous refrain of 'Hound Dog', attempting to swivel her non-existent hips while sneering at an ill-prepared world.

She pushed herself up off the counter. She seemed to be suspended in mid-air. It was a good place to be, she thought. She looked him deep in the eyes and said, "Yes, I believe I know exactly what she desires." She excused herself and floated behind the counter, reached into her bag below it, removed her diary, gift-wrapped it carefully, and handed it to Bono.

Hennessy Literary Awards
List Of Winners

Year	Winners
1971	Patrick Buckley, Kate Cruise O'Brien, Desmond Hogan, Vincent Lawrence, John Boland, Dermot Morgan, Liam Murphy
1972	Fred Johnston, Ita Daly, Maeve O'Brien Kelly, Patrick Cunningham
1973	John Flanagan, Niall MacSweeney, George O'Brien, Brian Power
1974	Donall MacAmhlaigh, Dermot Healy, John MacArdle, Ronan Sheehan
1975	Edward Brazil, Ray Lynott, Lucile Redmond, John A. Ryan
1976	Robin Glendinning, Ray Lynott, Ita Daly, Dermot Healy, Thomas O'Keefe, Sean O'Donovan
1977	Denis Byrne, Michael Feeney Callan, John O'Leary, Joseph Nesson
1978	Patrick Doyle, M. J. Lally, Jim Lusby, Andrew Tyrrell
1979	Mary O'Shea, Alan Stewart, Patrick McCabe, Harry McHugh
1980	David Irving, Paul Hyde, Deirdre Madden, Michael Harding
1981	Briege Duffaud, Catherine Coakley, Gabrielle Warnock, Elizabeth O'Driscoll

Hennessy Literary Awards
List Of Winners

Year	Winners
1982	Eoghan Power, Anne Devlin, Rose Doyle, Annette Gilmore
1983	Maurice Power, Jim McCarthy, Brigid Flaherty, John MacKenna
1984	Frances Dalton, Ronan O'Callaghan, Vincent Mahon, Bill Hearne
1985	Shane Connaughton, John Grenham, David Liddy, Brian Lynch
1986	Peter McNiff, Keith Collins, Andrew E. Duffy, Colm O'Clubhain
1987	Mary Byrne, Geraldine Meaney, Aine Miller, Mairide Woods
1988	Dermot Bolger, Maire Holmes, Ivy Bannister, James Leo Conway
1989	Joe O'Connor, Julian Girdham, Sam Burnside
1990	Colum McCann, Maeve Kennedy, Mary O'Malley
1991	Cathy O'Riordan, Colm Keena, Ted McNulty
1992	Mike Philpott, Mairide Woods, Sheila O'Hagan
1993	John Galvin, Mary Arrigan, Vona Groarke
1994	Marina Carr, Martin Healy, Noelle Vial

Hennessy Literary Awards
List Of Judges

Year	Judges
1971	Elizabeth Bowen, William Trevor
1972	Brian Friel, James Plunkett
1973	Sean O'Faolain, Kingsley Amis
1974	Edna O'Brien, V.S. Pritchett
1975	Brian Moore, William Saroyan
1976	Alan Stillitoe, Aidan Higgins
1977	Melvyn Bragg, John McGahern
1978	John Braine, Mary Lavin
1979	Julia O'Faolain, John Wain
1980	Bryan MacMahon, Penelope Mortimer
1981	Heinrich Boll, Terence de Vere White
1982	Jennifer Johnston, D.M. Thomas
1983	Victoria Glendinning, Benedict Kiely
1984	Molly Keane, John Mortimer
1985	Bernard MacLaverty, Robert Nye
1986	Frank Delaney, Judy Cooke
1987	Douglas Dunn, John Montague
1988	David Marcus, Ian McEwan

Hennessy Literary Awards
List Of Judges

Year	Judges
1989	Piers Paul Read, Brendan Kennelly
1990	Clare Boylan, Desmond Hogan
1991	Fay Weldon, Neil Jordan
1992	Wendy Cope, Hugh Leonard
1993	Penelope Lively, Ita Daly
1994	Beryl Bainbridge, Dermot Bolger